THE STUDY

A gripping murder mystery set in Canada

KATHY GARTHWAITE

Published by

The Book Folks

London, 2021

ISBN 978-1-913516-04-8

www.thebookfolks.com

Chapter 1

The first call came in at noon. Royal Canadian Mounted Police Sergeant Marlowe Flint was okay with that. It gave her a break from the paperwork she was working on. Although to be honest, she was barely listening as RCMP Corporal Naomi Thornberry rambled on about the ceremony she was attending at Crest Castle, a private residence that had been converted to a destination hotel by its current owner. The opening of a time capsule buried decades before promised to be the biggest event of the year.

Flint stood by the window in her office, more interested in the rollers crashing onto the beach below. The waves would grow taller and stronger as the days crept closer to winter. Soon, thrill seekers from every corner of the world would invade their pristine coast, like storm watchers, except they came to ride the waves. The previous day a rowdy crowd had partied into the late hours of the night and caused a flood of complaints from the sleepy inhabitants of Castlecrest on Vancouver Island, a coastal town shut in by the ancient rainforest surrounding it.

The sergeant muttered an occasional uh-huh in response to Thornberry's commentary about the ceremony as she stared out into the haze. Thin wisps of fog drifted lazily against the glass with the faintest brush of the wind. The slow sweep of a lighthouse lantern broke through the gloom at regular intervals. She took another sip of her coffee.

A low grumbling in the distance broke the peaceful moment. Flint caught a flash of red moving across the grey landscape, a motorcycle following the black ribbon of road that skirted the shoreline and wound its way to a point of land that jutted into the open water to a vague shape perched high on the bluff. The fog lifted somewhat, allowing a brief view of the castle. The mist curled around the stone structure, and then the vision vanished once again.

"Oh. Shit."

Thornberry's unexpected outburst made Flint start from her musings.

"What happened?" Flint asked.

"It's nothing. Just another delay," Thornberry said. "But if one more kid tries to squeeze by me, I'm going to put my foot out and trip them."

Flint heard some static on the line before the corporal spoke again.

"I wonder what the holdup is? If they don't hurry up, the mayor is going to run out of people to suck up to."

"He's just doing his job," Flint said.

"Yeah. Let me see. He was talking to an older man a minute ago. Now he's with someone at the podium. A good-looking woman."

"Don't be a jerk," Flint said.

"You guys are becoming a hot item," Thornberry said.

"What does the time capsule look like?" Flint asked, ignoring the last comment. After a fiasco with the fire chief in the summer, she thought that was the end of her romantic adventures for a bit. But the new mayor, Neil

Parson, had caught her eye as she did his. It had only been a short while, but things were going smoothly.

"They haven't brought it out yet. I'll keep you posted."

"Okay. Talk to you later," Flint said and hung up. She drained her mug and plunked down in her seat, wishing there wasn't always so much bureaucratic red tape. With barely enough time to shuffle around the folders on the table-top, she was interrupted by a chirp from her cell phone. She glanced at the screen and answered.

"Already? What have you got?"

"Oh my God. Harris is dead," Thornberry said.

"What?" Flint wasn't sure she heard that right.

"Harris—" The corporal's voice was interrupted by a strangled yelp.

"I have to go."

The line went dead.

Flint grabbed her jacket from the back of the chair and ran out of the station.

The breeze blowing off the cold waters of the Pacific Ocean had a bite as it swept over the ridge, rustling the last leaves remaining on the trees, and sent a shiver up her spine.

A foreboding of things to come.

Chapter 2

The castle appeared out of the mist as Flint drove up the blacktop road. As she approached the two-storey building, she saw brightly coloured canopies sprawled across an immense lawn that sloped down to the waterfront. It was pretty clear by the way the guests were mingling and laughing that they were unaware anything untoward had happened. Flint pulled into an elegant portico supported by tall white pillars and parked her car behind a police cruiser. The sound of trickling water from a fountain in the courtyard soothed her troubled thoughts. She hurried up the steps and entered a stunning entryway with a double curved staircase.

As sergeant, Flint headed the general investigation team that probed the serious crimes of robbery, rape and murder. She had been stationed in the homicide department with the Royal Canadian Mounted Police in Kelowna for ten years before taking a new position in her hometown. It was a perfect move, reuniting her with friends and family.

Her team consisted of a corporal and two constables. RCMP Constable Gordon Hay being the one she counted on the most. He had served the greatest part of his twenty-five years with the police force in the Province of Alberta. Neither the desolate landscape nor his position in the homicide department had hardened him to life. He was a jovial and exceptional officer. Corporal Thornberry was a young, sensible woman in her twenties who was still learning the ropes, but had become a valuable part of the team and a good friend.

Constable Hay stood guard at a door on the left side of the foyer, his duty belt loaded with handcuffs and baton hung low on his ample hips, waiting for her arrival.

"Sergeant. Thornberry is in here," Hay said as he opened the door. "Constable Patricia Greenwood is minding the other entrance."

"How is Patricia taking this?" Flint asked. Greenwood was the niece of the superintendent, on loan from Nanaimo to get some experience with hard crimes. The harbour city detachment was the major hub for the northern regions of the island with Superintendent Allen Gill as officer in charge of the entire district, including Castlecrest. He was Flint's boss.

Greenwood was covering for Constable Dennis Jarrett who was still on leave after taking a shot in the shoulder while on duty. Flint cringed at the thought, seeing as she felt responsible for the incident. She gritted her teeth, too much to do to think about that. It's in the past, best left alone.

"She's holding her own," Hay said.

"Good. I can't believe you guys got here so quickly."

"We were cruising this way when we got the call," Hay said and ran his hand through his thick grey hair.

"Right," Flint said. "How long did Dr. Kelly Churchman say it would take her to get here?"

"Any minute now," Hay said, then turned to the clacking of heels on the marble floor.

The pathologist from the BC Coroners Service was a tall, willowy woman. She was dressed in black pants and a cozy-looking cashmere sweater, carrying a small, black bag. A brief smile lit her face when she spotted the officers.

"Who's the victim?" she asked.

"Harris Crest. Mr. Charles Crest is his dad. He's the owner of this place," Hay said. "But we're not sure if it's an accident or not."

Flint glanced at the constable, wondering what they were doing here if it wasn't a murder.

"Well, let's take a look," the pathologist said and led the way into the study with the sergeant right behind her.

The highly polished wood panelling and oak desk gave the room a timeless quality. A few rugs scattered on the floors had deep, earthy colours that matched the aged leather settees. The built-in bookcase on the longest wall was crafted in the same classic style. Flint glanced at the titles printed on the spines of the books. Lodged among the journals and paperbacks, she spotted a number of first edition books. Her dad would love to see these, she thought.

Straight ahead, the floor-to-ceiling windows had a clear view of the ocean. Just to the right, an inconspicuous building nestled in a grove of giant fir trees was barely visible. Smoke curled effortlessly out of its chimney and drifted away with the breeze.

Thornberry stood by a chair that flanked a marble fireplace with an ornate tiled inset. She nodded to the sergeant who turned her attention to the young man sprawled on the floor. His limp body leaned awkwardly on its side with his head rested against the stone hearth. The crisp, white shirt he wore had stains from the drops of blood that trickled off his earlobe.

The pathologist knelt beside the prone figure and started her examination.

Flint glanced back when the corporal cleared her throat.

"The crime scene unit and the photographer are on their way," Thornberry said.

"Thanks." Flint walked over to the window and pressed her face against the glass but couldn't see the canopies.

She rapped her knuckles against the pane to get Greenwood to look in her direction. The soft brown eyes that greeted the sergeant had a hint of disquiet in them. Flint gave her a nod and turned back into the room.

"So, what was the noise I heard over the phone?" Flint asked.

"Oh, that was Charles Crest. He came through the patio doors just as Hay and I arrived at the scene. He saw his son lying on the ground and freaked out. It caught us off guard. We practically had to pry him off." Thornberry puckered her lips in dismay.

"That's unfortunate. Where is he now?"

"Paulie took him back to his cottage and fetched his doctor," Thornberry said.

"Who's his doctor?"

"Dr. Chester Lane."

"Right. I know him," Flint said.

"Charles walked out of here on his own. He kept slapping at Paulie to leave him alone," Thornberry said. "Amazing. I think the old man must be a hundred years old."

"Well, he's ninety something anyway. He has grit, that's for sure. Did he say anything?"

"No. He just cried out and fell down on his knees."

"Did he touch the body?"

"I'm afraid so," Thornberry said. "Hopefully, he didn't contaminate any evidence."

"The forensic team will sort that out," Flint said. She looked at Thornberry quizzically. "By the way, who's Paulie?"

"He's the new manager."

"Of course. Mr. Webb. He runs the entire hotel. Right?"

"Yeah, I think so."

"Was it Paulie who discovered the body then?"

"No, a waitress did. Mia Shaw. She's in the staff medical clinic at the back of the building. Apparently, she had just popped her head in to see if Harris wanted a cup of coffee or something," Thornberry said.

"Okay. And then what happened?"

"She told the manager, and he came and got me," Thornberry said. "We had spoken earlier, so he knew where I was sitting."

"This was no accident," Churchman said. She stood up and faced the detectives.

"Okay. What have you got?" Flint asked.

"Those cuts on his hands and arms are defensive wounds." The pathologist held up her hands in front of her face. "Like this. The victim was trying to protect his face and upper body from the attack. It's interesting that the cuts are mostly superficial."

"So the victim was attacked with a knife," Flint said.

"Yes. There was probably a little scuffle. The victim fell backward and hit his head on the hearth. I can't tell you whether the attacker meant to kill him or just scare him. That's something for you to figure out."

"Fair enough," Flint said.

"I would say the impact on the stone is the cause of death. I can't see anything else." Churchman pointed to the gash on the side of Harris's head. "But I will confirm everything when I do the autopsy. I'll get on it as soon as I can." She packed up her bag.

"Okay, thanks," Flint said.

The pathologist turned at the doorway. "I'll give you a shout."

Flint looked around the room. Her eyes landed on the desk where various articles were stacked and arranged neatly around each other with the capsule in the centre. The stainless-steel cylinder had a pleasing, soft metallic patina. It was larger than she thought it would be, almost a foot across and two feet tall.

"Pretty nice," Thornberry said. "So was there something in it that the killer wanted? Some secret from the past?"

"You're being a bit melodramatic, don't you think?" Flint asked.

"Maybe there was some rare or expensive heirloom," Thornberry persisted.

"Well, that's something we'll have to look into," Flint said. She gazed at the items on the table. "Nothing here looks that valuable. Nothing I would want particularly."

"Well, I suppose our guy got what he came for," Thornberry said. "The rest is just old stuff."

"Maybe."

"Gold coins, diamonds. Those are always handy."

"I get your point," Flint said.

The detectives looked up at the sound of the door opening.

"Hello, ladies," Ryan Harper said as he stepped into the room, his bag of tricks in his right hand.

The crime scene investigator was a forensic scientist with fourteen years of field experience. He specialized in fingerprints and weapons. His office was just a few doors down from their department, although he spent a great deal of time at the RCMP crime lab at the Nanaimo station where all potential evidence was submitted.

"Hi, there. Dr. Churchman has been and gone," Flint said. "We're just waiting for the photographer."

"Is she on her way?" Ryan asked.

Just then a young lady, all of a hundred pounds, appeared at the door. She was dressed in jeans and a sweater with untied running shoes on her feet.

"I know, I'm late," the photographer said.

"Come in," Flint said.

"Sorry, I had the kids with me when I got the call," Suzy said. She stumbled into the room, overburdened with bags and cameras slung over her shoulders. She placed her equipment on the floor hurriedly. "I'll get on with it then. Shall I?"

"No problem," Flint said and turned to Ryan. "Where's your help today?"

"I'm on my own."

"We'll leave you to it then," Flint said.

"I'll let you know what I find," Ryan said.

"You bet," Flint said.

Ryan set his bag down next to the fireplace and set to work, trying to stay out of Suzy's way.

"All right. Time to round up some witnesses," Flint said.

"Let's do it," Thornberry said.

Hay stood on the far side of the yellow and black tape that had been strung around the crime scene.

"Looks like you have everything under control here," Flint said as she slipped under the tape.

"Two officers are on their way to watch over the crime scene until Ryan is done," Hay said. "Greenwood will meet us up front."

"Good work," Flint said.

"There's quite the turnout today," Hay said. "Must be a hundred people."

"Locals only invite," Thornberry said.

"Oh, shit," Flint said.

"What?" Thornberry asked. "You think it's one of them?"

"That would be logical," Hay said.

"You mean it could be someone we know?" Thornberry asked.

"Someone we know," Flint repeated.

Chapter 3

Although the fog had lifted, there was still a chill in the air. A low autumn light cast long shadows across the grass. The detectives waited at the front entrance for the constable to show up.

In a few long strides, Greenwood skipped around the corner of the building and stopped in front of them. She pushed the blonde side sweep of bangs that contrasted starkly with her short black hair away from her face. Her cheeks were flushed a rosy-pink blossom.

"Here I am," Greenwood said. "What's next?"

"I guess I better make a brief statement before the crowd gets wind of this," Flint said. "Don't want to cause a panic."

As she spoke, the sirens of an ambulance could be heard heading their way. Soon the flashing lights came into view.

"No time to waste now," Flint said. "Come on."

They strode up to the raised platform and ascended the stairs in single file. Flint stood behind the podium while her team lined up behind her.

"Could I have your attention, please? Quiet, everyone. Please, have a seat."

Flint waited a few minutes before she spoke again.

"I have an announcement to make. Some bad news, I'm afraid. There has been an accident. Harris Crest has died as a result of that. For those who don't know, Harris is the hotel owner's son," Flint said.

She looked around the people assembled together for the event before she continued.

"Now I don't want anyone to panic. There is no reason to be alarmed. You are not in any danger. This will be a little difficult to take in, but Harris was murdered."

She stopped to allow the murmur to die down.

"Okay. Settle down. I don't have any details to give you at this time, but we could use your help. If anyone saw anything suspicious, we ask you to step forward. We will be setting up an interview room." She turned toward Hay. He whispered in her ear. "If you would like to speak to us, please report to the officer who will be stationed at the front entrance."

An even noisier buzz erupted.

"Please, everyone. Let me finish. Before you leave the premises, we'll need everybody's contact information. Be patient while a table is assembled at the front here to expedite the process. Please be orderly, and we'll get through this quickly. We will be in contact with each and every one of you over the next few days to get a statement. Be assured, we'll be conducting an exhaustive inquiry into this matter. We will find out who did this. Thank you for your co-operation," Flint said.

There was a stunned silence.

"I won't be answering any questions at this time." Flint thrust the microphone aside and walked off the platform.

"That was good," Hay said.

"Let's get out of here before we get mobbed," Flint said.

The room Hay had arranged for them was twice as large as the study. It had the same magnificent woodwork and old fir floors. Probably milled from trees when the property was cleared for building, Flint thought. Everything about the castle was first-class, the structure itself, the magnificent gardens, the service when it turned into a hotel. But now it would be marred by a murder in the study. That would never go away.

"What about the guests staying at the hotel?" Flint asked after they had seated themselves around the oval table.

"I checked at the receptionist desk. There are no guests at the moment," Hay said. "The hotel was closed down for this ceremony. But they do have bookings for tomorrow, and the dining room will be re-opened."

"So let's get back to who discovered the body," Flint said. "So you said Mia, one of the waitresses, found Harris. Okay, we should–" Flint was interrupted by a soft tapping.

A middle-aged lady dressed in a red ankle-length skirt and a patterned blouse with puffy sleeves stood in the doorway.

"I'm sorry to interrupt. I was told to come here. I saw something."

"Come in," Hay said.

"Okay." She pulled her shawl tighter around her shoulders and took a seat next to the constable.

"Thanks for coming. Can we get your name first?" Flint asked.

"Leanne Abbot."

"Can you tell us what you saw then?"

Leanne hesitated. "Honestly, I don't know if this will help."

"Everything helps, so go ahead," Flint said.

"I saw someone running from the side of the building."

"What time was this?" Flint asked.

"Well, I don't know the time exactly. First I saw the man running, and then fifteen minutes later I saw Charles Crest coming up the slope."

"So what was this man wearing?" Flint asked. She leaned forward and placed her elbows on the table.

"I'm not sure. Jeans, I think."

"Was this person tall or short? Fat or thin?" Flint pursued her line of questioning. Any detail would be useful.

"Maybe tall. It's hard to tell. Sorry. I probably just wasted your time." She frowned.

"Not at all. Thank you. If anything else comes to mind give me a call," Flint said. She handed the lady a card. "Even if it doesn't seem important to you."

"Okay." Leanne stood up. "Sorry."

After the lady left, Flint flopped back into her chair. "Well, at least we know which way the killer went." She held up her hand when Thornberry was about to object. "It fits the timeline. A person is seen running, then Charles enters the study and finds his son dead." She turned to Hay. "Did you check for cameras?"

"They don't have cameras in or around the castle."

"Really?" Flint crossed her arms and looked around the room. "Doesn't look like we have a rush of witnesses coming forward, either."

There was a knock at the door and Ryan popped his head in.

"Am I interrupting?"

"Not at all," Flint said. "What have you got for us?"

"I don't have a lot of good news. Well, any news really. There are plenty of prints in the study. Too many. Probably won't be of any help. Lots of people come and go out of there," Ryan said. "The blood on the hearth is probably just from the victim. But I won't leave that to chance. I will get the samples tested. As far as the capsule and its contents go, I will personally go over that myself."

"That's slim pickings," Flint said.

"Yeah," Ryan said. "There might be some evidence on the victim's clothing. I should get those by tomorrow." The forensic scientist ran his hand over the stubble on his chin. "I'm headed over to the lab now." He turned to leave and bumped into a tall man standing in the doorway, a black medical bag clutched in one hand. The man pulled a cap from his head, revealing a messy mop of dark, curly hair.

"Chester. Haven't seen you in a while," Ryan said. They shook hands.

"Dr. Lane. What can we do for you?" Flint asked.

"Hello. I heard you were here. I just wanted to let you know that Charles is quite upset. His wife died of cancer a few months ago. Now this. So I am a bit worried for his health," the doctor said. "Look. He has a bad ticker so could you be easy on him?"

"Absolutely, we will. Don't worry," Flint said. "Thanks for letting us know."

"Okay, then. How are things going? Any suspects?"

"It's too early to say, but we have some leads," Flint said.

"Oh, good. Charles will be happy with that," Dr. Lane said. "I best be going."

Ryan placed his hand on the doctor's shoulder. "I'll walk out with you."

"It's a terrible situation," Dr. Lane said.

"How are things going otherwise?" Ryan asked.

Their voices faded as they walked away.

"Dr. Lane goes the distance," Flint said. "Even the thing with his wife didn't change him."

"What was that?" Greenwood asked.

"His wife just up and left him and the kid one day," Flint said. "That was a long time ago. His kid must be a teenager now."

"Whoa," Greenwood said.

"Yeah. I know Shawn. He's been in a few scraps at the community centre where I volunteer. Nothing serious," Thornberry said. "I saw him earlier in the parking lot with a bunch of kids having a smoke. Maybe it was a joint. Who knows these days? It's legal now. Although, it never stopped them before."

"Okay, we're getting off topic. Let's get back on track," Flint said, cutting into her corporal's ramblings. "Hay. I want you and Thornberry to search the grounds. Chiefly you'll be looking for the knife that the killer used. If the person was smart, they would have stashed it someplace where it could most easily be retrieved at a later stage because if we find it, game over. Right? Concentrate your efforts in the area from the patio doors down toward the waterfront. Check under shrubs, in garbage bins, anywhere someone could possibly conceal a weapon. You know the drill. Get a couple of uniforms to help with the search."

"And then go from there? Right, boss?" Hay asked. "We don't know which direction the killer took after the lady lost sight of him."

"That goes without saying. Widen your search. I want the knife."

"We'll do our best," Hay said.

"We have plenty to do. So let's get cracking. Greenwood, you're with me. I think the first order of business is to have a chat with the manager. Where do you think we'll find him?"

"If I was him, I would hide out in my office," Greenwood said. "Having a murder on your watch is never good."

"Yeah. Wait until he finds out the time capsule is off-limits for a while," Flint said. "That won't sit right with him, I'm sure."

"Bad day gone worse."

The detectives walked toward the back of the building. High ceilings, graceful archways, decorative coving and polished timber floors of the period gave a feeling of grandeur. Greenwood was astonished at the sheer opulence, the extravagant spending of the wealthy.

"Holy shit, Charles must be loaded," Greenwood said. "Look at all this shit."

Flint frowned and wondered if the murder was all about the money somehow.

They walked past several closed doors before they found one marked 'Office'.

Flint knocked lightly and jiggled the handle, but it was locked.

"Where else could he be?"

When they heard the distinct clink of metal from behind the heavy oak door, the detectives looked at each other.

Chapter 4

The day had lost its heat, leaving a dull sun and a fresh crispness. A smoke smell drifted in through the open window and hung in the air. The sweet aroma had hints of pine and maple.

The manager sat behind his desk, thinking about what he had done. Fear stopped him from taking the key out of his pocket. He glanced at the door several times. Yes, he had locked it, no one could barge in on him.

Paulie fingered the metal, cold to the touch, the raised image smooth beneath his fingertips. Slowly, he withdrew the key and held it up in the darkened room. He switched on the lamp behind him. If he squinted, he could just make out the shape of small, round balls and a sword. He wasn't sure what they meant exactly. As he pulled the key in closer, an embossed pattern revealed itself on the other side. Just what he had hoped for, the Crest family emblem.

He twirled the key in his hand, his eyes bright with anticipation. The object he had sought and now secured would unlock something special. Something valuable. He chuckled. It was almost laughable how easily it had come into his possession. As if it was inevitable.

A knock on the door startled Paulie out of his thoughts, the sound seeming louder and more threatening than usual. He lost his grip on the key, and it dropped onto the desk with a loud clunk. He froze, waiting, wondering if he had been discovered. He held his breath, quiet as a mouse, listening, but there were no more sounds. He shoved the key back into his pocket, mixed emotions of nervousness and reassurance making him dizzy.

The second knock was louder, more ominous.

"Coming," he shouted out, his voice cracking.

Flint glanced at Greenwood and raised her eyebrows.

There was a click and the door opened.

The dishevelled middle-aged man standing in the doorway looked tired; large dark circles underneath his eyes, in spite of the large smile plastered on his face.

"Mr. Paulie Webb?"

"Yes, how may I help you?"

"I'm Sergeant Flint. This is Constable Greenwood. May we have a moment of your time?"

"Yes, of course, I've been expecting someone from the police," Paulie said as he stepped aside. "Have a seat."

The room was uncomfortably small and cramped with three gunmetal grey filing cabinets against one wall protruding into the space. The old wood panelling and dark herringbone floor closed the walls in further. The only redeeming feature was a large window that overlooked the forest to the north.

Paulie strode back behind his desk and folded his hands on the surface. The detectives sat on hard high-backed chairs across from him. Greenwood pulled a notebook and pen from her jacket pocket.

"Tell me, how long have you been manager here?" Flint asked.

"Going on six months," Paulie said. He smiled widely.

"I imagine you know the ropes by now."

"That's true."

"You run the whole show? You don't have an assistant?" Flint asked.

"I'm totally in charge of the entire operation," Paulie said. His eyes narrowed at the insinuation. "I'm highly qualified."

"Quite," Flint said. "So if there was an issue, an employee would feel that they could come to you?"

"Naturally, they would seek me out to solve their problem. My office is an open door."

Flint glanced out the window. Well, why was it locked when we got here, she thought. "So Mia would search for you, rather than stop the first person she ran into? Even under the circumstances?"

"Are you suggesting I had something to do with this?"

"Not at all, Mr. Webb," Flint said. "So–"

"Look, Mia came up to me and told me Harris was hurt," Paulie interrupted. "So I hurried to the study. One look and I knew he was dead. I wasted no time and sought out that other officer I had spoken to earlier."

"You mean, Corporal Thornberry?"

"Yes, that's right."

"Okay. That's good," Flint said. "Now, I'm a little confused about why the time capsule was dug up. It's only been buried for forty years. Was that the plan all along?"

"That's not my department."

"Really?" Flint shot him a look, thinking he had just said he was in charge of everything.

"It was Harris who made that decision. It's outside of my job description." Paulie pushed his thumbs together.

"Have you got any ideas why? I know it was sudden," Flint said, deciding not to get into a war of words with the guy. "I only heard about it a few weeks ago myself."

"Why? Do you think the time capsule has something to do with Harris's death?"

"I can't get into that," Flint said. "So do you know what his reasoning was?"

"Maybe it has something to do with the property line. There were rumours," Paulie said.

"What kind of rumours?"

"A dispute about the land. I'm not really sure what it's all about. Ask Bryson Williams. He's the real estate developer next door," Paulie said.

"Could you be more specific?"

"Not really. Ask Bryson. I'm kept in the dark about a lot of things around here," Paulie said. "It makes me mad. Do you have any idea how hard it is to run a place as large as this under those circumstances? It would be nice to know if Bryson plans to go ahead with his hotel."

"Was there some antagonism between you and Harris? Did you quarrel?"

"No. Don't put words in my mouth," Paulie said. He shuffled uneasily in his chair. "I just feel I should be kept in the loop about everything. Apparently, I'm not. But it doesn't really matter, I have plenty to do."

"Is there anything else that we should know?" Flint asked.

"Sorry, I didn't mean to spout off. If I think of anything else..."

"Thanks for your cooperation," Flint said. "You were very helpful."

"Okay," Paulie said. "What about the time capsule? When can I get that back?"

"It's evidence, so it could be a while."

"What am I supposed to do now?" Paulie asked. "People have booked into the hotel just to see it."

"We'll let you know."

"Okay. Just another problem." He sighed. "I'll figure out something."

"Where is the medical clinic?" Flint asked. She stood up, towering over the desk.

"Yeah, it's at the very back. You can't miss it."

"Thanks."

Flint closed the door behind them. She heard the click of the lock.

The detectives passed the kitchen on their way. The usual loud chatter of dishes was missing. Only a few people were working. Others stood around gossiping. Everyone would have heard the news by now.

"He was nervous. Don't you think?" Greenwood asked.

"Maybe a little," Flint said.

"Is there some connection between a land dispute, the time capsule and the murder?"

"Well, that's something we'll have to explore," Flint said. She stopped in front of the clinic, knocked on the door and entered.

The room was painted a soft green. Chrome and leather chairs lined either side of the space with a reception area at the end. It didn't have the same feel of poshness as the rest of the castle but was clean and modern.

There wasn't anybody to greet them, so Flint rang the bell on the counter. A girl in her mid-twenties dressed in a nurse's uniform scurried from the back.

"How may I help you?"

"I would like a moment with Mia, if that is possible?" Flint flashed her badge.

"I was just going to pack her off home," the nurse said. "She's in the first cubicle on the right. Go ahead."

"Thanks." Flint glanced at Greenwood and tilted her chin toward the row of chairs along one wall.

The constable sat down to wait.

"Hello. I'm the investigating sergeant. May I have a word with you?" Flint said through the closed curtain.

"Come in," Mia replied after a short hesitation.

The sergeant pushed back the cloth and sat on a chair beside the bed.

"Are you doing okay? I know that must have been quite the shock finding Harris the way you did."

"That was horrible. Poor Harris," Mia said. Her eyes were red and swollen. "What happened?"

"That's what I want to talk to you about," Flint said. "I understand you found Harris on the floor and called for help. What were you doing there?"

"I was just going to ask him if he wanted a coffee or something," Mia said. "I had been quite busy all morning setting up the refreshments. I didn't think Harris had left the room all that time. I thought he might appreciate a drink."

"That was nice of you."

"Yeah, I guess."

"Was the door open or did you have to knock?" Flint asked.

"It was partially open, so I tapped on the door and let myself in," Mia said. "I wish I hadn't." Her face paled.

"Had you noticed if the door was open all morning?" Flint carried on with her questions instead of lingering on the one thing that would stick in the girl's mind forever.

"I think so." Mia scrunched up her face. "It must have been, because otherwise I wouldn't have disturbed him."

"Did you hear Harris talking to anyone when you passed by the study at any time this morning?"

"No."

"Did you step into the room or just stand in the doorway?"

"No, I didn't go in. I saw Harris on the ground and turned away. My heart was going a hundred kilometres an hour," Mia said. "I bumped into Mr. Webb in the foyer and told him what I saw."

"Mr. Webb was close by then?"

"Yes. I turned around and there he was. Thank goodness."

"Did Mr. Webb go into the study?"

"Just for a moment."

"What did you do when he went into the study? Did you follow him?"

"No way. I waited in the foyer," Mia said. "Was I supposed to do something?" A tear ran down her cheek. She swiped it away with the back of her hand.

"Not at all. What happened next?"

"Paulie asked me to stand by the door until he returned with a policeman."

"Did that make you nervous to be there alone?"

"Are you kidding? I was so scared," Mia said.

"That was very brave of you," Flint said. "Did you think Harris was injured badly?"

"I thought he was dead," Mia said. "I think Mr. Webb thought so too."

"So how much time passed before the manager came back?" Flint asked.

"It felt like a lifetime, but it was probably just six or seven minutes."

"Okay. Did a police officer come along with him?"

"Not that I saw."

"What did you do next?" Flint asked.

"Mr. Webb sent me to the clinic," Mia said. "I was happy to be out of there, I tell you."

"Is there anything else you can think of?"

"No, not really," Mia said. "Well, I looked back and saw a chubby lady I didn't know go in the study. Maybe that was the police officer."

Flint figured that was Thornberry. She handed the girl her card. "If you remember anything else, no matter how trivial you think it is, please call me. Could you do that for me?"

"Yeah, sure." Mia took the card and placed it in a pocket. "Harris is dead, isn't he?"

"Yes, I'm sorry to say."

"Okay." Mia cast her eyes down to the ground and brushed her hands down her skirt.

"You take care," Flint said. She walked out of the cubicle and thanked the nurse.

"Let's grab something to eat," Flint said to Greenwood.

"Sure."

After a detour to the take-out window, the detectives walked slowly towards the front entrance munching on their sandwiches.

"So what did Mia have to say? Anything interesting?" Greenwood asked in between bites.

"Maybe."

"Like what?"

"After Mia discovered Harris, she ran into Paulie who was just outside the door of the study," Flint said.

"Was it a coincidence that he was right there?"

"I'm curious why he lied to us," Flint said. "I think we better expand our search to inside the building."

"Really?" Greenwood asked. "Why?"

"I'm beginning to wonder who wasn't in the study this morning," Flint said as she furrowed her eyebrows in displeasure. "We assumed the man running from the building was the killer. Now I'm not so sure."

Chapter 5

Flint and Greenwood headed across the lawn. As they crested the slope, a group of older buildings came into view. The downward grade was not as steep but levelled out smoothly to the beach. Three white-washed cottages, separated by gravel paths, had short picket fences surrounding the tidy gardens out front. Paulie had told them Charles lived in the one closest to the water beside a copse of trees. A honeysuckle vine trailed from the corner of the house and draped over the entrance, its leaves mostly on the ground now. At the side, black garbage cans and a propane tank could be seen through the fretwork of a lattice panel.

Irish moss grew in the crevices of the old winding flagstone path. The air was scented with the sweetness of pansies from a basket hanging off a beam. Flint rapped the door knocker softly, not wanting to disturb the grieving father in case he was napping.

"Come in," someone growled.

A sudden blast of warmth hit them when Flint opened the door. The room had wooden panelling and a brick fireplace with a bookcase on either side. Flint noticed the photos first, a boy and a woman, grown older over the decades in each subsequent picture. Harris and his mom. The books and journals were a mishmash of titles which ranged from spy novels to local lore.

Charles sat in one of the large, comfortable chairs in front of a fire blazing brightly.

"Who are you?" He didn't move in his seat but stared straight ahead, his rheumy eyes sunken, his lips parched.

"I hope we're not bothering you at such a distressing time. I'm Sergeant Flint from the RCMP. This is Constable Greenwood. May we come in for a moment?"

"Of course you're bothering me. My son was just killed," Charles said.

"We'll be short."

"I suppose I have no choice." He turned his head and looked at the detectives. "May as well have a seat." He gestured to the other chairs in front of the fireplace.

"Thank you," Flint said. She sat on a deep-cushioned chair while Greenwood chose a seat at the kitchen table.

"May we offer our sincerest condolences," Flint said.

"Yeah, yeah." Charles waved her off.

"Did Harris have any enemies? Can you think who might have done this?" Flint asked.

"Nobody would want to hurt Harris even if he rubbed people the wrong way sometimes."

"Who would that–" Flint started.

Charles let out an agonized cry of pain as tears rolled down his cheeks.

Flint glanced sideways at Greenwood.

The old man stirred in his chair, struggling to sit up straight.

"Maybe we should come back tomorrow," Flint said.

Charles sighed. "No, I'm okay. Ask me your questions."

"When was the last time you saw your son?"

"This morning," Charles said. "I saw him head up to the castle about nine."

"Did you speak with him?"

"No." The old man's eyes welled up again. He held the tears back.

"I understand that Harris decided to dig out the time capsule early. Is that correct?"

"Yes."

"Was it because of the development next door?" Flint asked. Paulie had hinted that much.

"I think the capsule might have been on the property line. But I'm not sure why it mattered now and not before. It was all Harris. Not me. Not Bryson."

Charles stared into the fire.

Flint kept silent.

"Harris would still be alive if he had let it be," Charles said. He slumped back into his chair, his breathing laboured.

"Can I get you some water?" Flint asked. She perched on the edge of her seat and leaned forward. This was the last thing she needed. Another incident.

"No. Get me a whisky." He pointed to a sideboard. "Over there."

Greenwood rushed over and poured a generous measure into a crystal tumbler. She placed it on the table beside the old man.

He gave her an approving nod and took a deep sip. "That's better."

The heat in the room was becoming distracting, but Flint had him talking so she carried on.

"What was the original date for the capsule to be dug out?" Flint asked, trying to get back to the original question.

"It was to stay in the ground for fifty years."

"So let me get this straight. Nobody forced Harris to dig up the capsule. He did it of his own accord. Did he give you a reason?"

"Harris just always did what he wanted. And to be honest, we always let him. We spoiled him." Charles looked wistfully into the fire.

"What did you think?"

"Nothing. If Harris wanted to dig it up, well..." He trailed off and shrugged.

"Did you put anything in the capsule?"

"No." Charles eyed the sergeant and pursed his lips.

"Okay. So everything was set up for guests. After Harris made a speech, he was going to open it," Flint said. She had the feeling that the old man had some stake in the contents of the capsule. It also made her think about why the capsule was already opened. She had seen the contents on the desk.

"That's what he told me."

"What was your schedule this morning? Did you go up and take a look?"

"No. I sat out in my back garden most of the morning. I headed up there after lunch. I wasn't in the mood to mingle. Damn fools gushing all over the place. Just wanted to get the ceremony over with. I wasn't really happy about the whole thing." Charles shrugged. "But like I said, it was what Harris wanted and I went along with it."

"Did you go to the guest area first?" Flint asked, although she knew he went straight to the study.

"I was going to, but I noticed the capsule wasn't there yet. So I went to see what was taking so long. I didn't want to be out all day. I have my afternoon nap to consider."

"I see. So you walked up to the study. Did you see anybody on the way there?"

"No."

"Was the door of the study open or closed?"

"It was opened a crack."

"So you went right in?"

"Of course I did. I own the place."

"Tell me what you did next."

"I saw the capsule on the desk. It was already opened. I have no idea why. I thought the idea was to have the great unveiling." Charles used his fingers to emphasize his point. "I didn't see Harris right away. At first, I thought he had already left." He cleared his throat. "Then I stepped further into the room. Oh, my God. I didn't know what had happened. But..." He choked back a sob.

"Hang on a minute. Take a deep breath."

"I'm okay. Don't fuss," Charles said.

Flint waited so he could continue at his own pace.

"I went over to him to see if he was okay. To check his pulse. The next thing I knew the room was full of people," Charles said. "Paulie walked with me back to my house. Then he left to fetch my doctor. I didn't want him to call Lane, but these young fellows are so damn pushy. I just sat in my chair and let them do what they wanted." He fell back deeper into the cushion.

"Thank you for your time. We're really sorry about Harris," Flint said. She figured they had learned all they were going to for the moment. The old man needed to rest.

"Me, too." Charles pulled his sweater tighter to his thin frame. "Could you stoke the fire before you leave? I missed my nap time."

"Of course." Flint threw on another log from the cradle on the hearth and poked at the embers. When she turned around, Charles's eyes were closed. There was an audible wheeze as he breathed in and out. He was an old man who had lost everything that counted. She glanced at the photos one more time and turned away.

The detectives slipped out of the cottage and stood on the small porch.

"I'm not sure what part the capsule plays in our investigation," Flint said.

"I think there was something in it that Harris wanted," Greenwood said.

"Maybe," Flint said. "We have conflicting opinions on whether Bryson is involved. Paulie said he was. Charles says no." She looked up at the castle silhouetted against the darkening evening sky. Two figures emerged from the shadows.

"We found something," Hay said.

Chapter 6

"You found the knife?" Greenwood asked.

"No, a pair of secateurs," Hay said. He held up an evidence bag with the red-handled pruners inside. "They obviously belong to someone from the garden staff."

"Where does that get us exactly?" Flint asked. She tried not to show her disappointment.

"I'm thinking a witness," Hay said.

"Sorry, but I'm not following you."

"I found them in the garden bed under the study window."

"How do we know they were dropped there this morning?" Flint asked.

"The soil was freshly turned, and there were packs of pansies in a tray not yet planted. Like someone had intended to return," Hay said, turning the packet over in his hands.

"Okay, that makes sense." Flint paused. "It shouldn't be hard to find out who was working there."

"Someone has scratched their initials on the side." Hay pointed. "JJ."

"Even better. Do we have a list of staff?" Flint asked.

"No. I'll get it first thing in the morning," Hay said.

"Okay. So you think whoever dropped these might have heard something?" Flint asked. She took the pruners and ran her finger along the initials.

"Or they saw the killer," Hay said.

"Well, that's a scary thought."

"Exactly. That could be why they didn't come forward. They got scared."

"Or they knew the person," Thornberry said.

"Jesus. We better find this person right away before something else happens," Flint said.

"What? You're thinking the killer saw them?" Hay asked.

"Maybe. But let's not get ahead of ourselves." Flint eyed her team. They looked exhausted both physically and mentally. "Go home and get a good rest. Tomorrow will be another long day."

"Aren't you coming?" Thornberry turned around after starting up the hill.

"I'm just going to take a look around the garden shed," Flint said.

"You sure?" Hay asked. "It's getting dark."

"Don't worry. I'm right behind you." Flint shuddered just slightly and pressed her hand against the flashlight on her duty belt. "I'm fine."

"Okay. See you in the morning," Hay said.

Flint watched them trudge up the slope. She turned toward the building she had seen earlier from the study window. As she approached the shed, she noticed the smoke that had been belching from the chimney earlier had died down to a thin wispy haze. Although there were no lights on inside, she rattled the door anyway but it was locked. Everyone had gone home for the day.

Flint peered through the forest toward the water. But the tall fir trees cut off most of the light from the sun that was slowly slipping below the horizon, leaving an inky blackness.

A sudden panic made her heart skip a beat. It took only a moment. A fear of the dark Flint had not quite mastered and always caught her unexpectedly took hold of her now. It bore down on her and nipped at her heels as she hurried back up the slope, her flashlight all but forgotten bouncing off her hip. She broke into a run, desperately trying to reach the castle. With the last of her energy almost depleted, she rounded the corner of the building and stood at the hood of her vehicle under the bright lights of the portico. She placed her hands on her thighs and took slow deep breaths to stop the thudding of her racing heart.

Flint slid into the driver's seat and hit the steering wheel with her palm. "Damn." She pushed her head against the rest and closed her eyes. A ping from her cell phone sounded. She looked at the screen and answered.

"Superintendent Gill."

"Don't go all formal on me. It's Allen."

"I was just going to phone–" Flint started.

"Don't worry. The grapevine is loud and long-reaching."

"Sorry, sir," Flint said. "I should have called earlier."

"I know how these things go. I'm sure it's been a long day for everyone there," Gill said. "But there is one thing I would like to make clear."

"Okay."

"The Crest family is important to this community," Gill said. "Use all the resources you want to get this investigation finalized. Are you hearing me?"

"That goes without saying."

"Good. I'm sure you'll get it done."

"We're doing our best," Flint said. "We won't let up."

"That's what I want to hear," Gill said. "How's Charles holding up?"

"As best as can be expected under the circumstances."

"I'll give him a shout tomorrow. Let him know we won't leave any stone unturned."

"Absolutely."

"Keep me updated," Gill said. "And get some sleep."

"Yes, sir. Will do."

The superintendent hung up.

Flint heaved a sigh of relief. She had completely forgotten to call the boss. Her cell pinged again. She answered immediately.

"Flint."

"Is this the person in charge of the investigation? You know. About Harris?"

The voice was squeaky, a young person unsure of themself.

"Yes. How can I help you? Miss...?" Flint asked.

"It's Kim Weaver. I'm a waitress in the dining room at the castle." She paused. "Well, today I had to leave in a hurry because I broke my finger."

"Okay."

"Well, you see, I'm phoning because I heard what happened with Harris."

"So you haven't been interviewed by an officer yet?"

"No. I only just heard about it a few moments ago."

"What can you tell me?" Flint asked. "Did you see something?"

"Like I said, I was leaving to go to the hospital when somebody came running out of the study and nearly knocked me down," Kim said.

"What time was this?" Flint sat up, ears alert like her dog.

"Just before noon. Maybe closer to eleven thirty," Kim said. "I'm not sure. There was blood everywhere." She stopped, inhaling deeply. "Sorry that was stupid. I meant from my finger."

"Do you know the person who ran into you?" Flint asked.

"Sort of."

"Could you expand on that?"

"I think it was a councillor," Kim said.

"You're not sure?"

"I saw his picture in the paper about the development next door," Kim said. "I just don't know his name."

"Would be able to pick him out from the photo then?"

"Yeah, sure," Kim said.

Flint heard the girl clear her throat.

"Come to think of it, maybe the guy was the mayor not a councillor," Kim said.

Flint leaned back into her seat.

"Okay, leave this with me. Give me your number. I'll arrange for you to take another look at that picture tomorrow," Flint said. "Thanks for calling in."

"No problem," Kim said and hung up.

Flint started up the engine and headed home. She knew the photo that Kim was talking about. It was on the front page of the local paper a while ago. She thought back. There were several councillors, the mayor and the real estate guy standing in a row. She had made fun of Neil, acting like a big shot and all. Now it didn't seem so funny. Her last boyfriend was in jail for murder. Was this a new trend for her? Had she made another mistake in her choice of men? How well did she even know Neil? After all, he was new in town. She swallowed the lump in her throat, feeling a little ill.

* * *

The large two-storey house built in the 1900s had a steep pitched roof and white shingle cladding. Flint parked in the driveway behind her dad's vehicle. She looked up to the dormer window where Paige was tucked into her bed, right next door to her room through a Jack and Jill bathroom. Flint had been raised here and she felt a great relief that her own daughter was growing up in the same loving environment.

Flint slipped quietly in the back door and was greeted with a swish of a tail against the wood floor.

"Good boy."

The golden retriever's ears perked up, anticipating the next word.

"Walkies. Give me ten." Flint gently ran her hand down the dog's thick fur coat.

She made herself a cup of tea and headed to the living room where her dad would be ensconced in a book, probably one of his first edition novels. She stood in the doorway a few minutes, immediately struck by the sense of peace in the room. Victor Sullivan sat in his favourite chair, a blanket across his knees and a roaring fire chasing away the dampness.

"Hi, Dad."

"Hello, sweetheart." Victor placed his book on the table by his elbow.

Flint smirked. *No Country For Old Men*. The book was bound in quarter red morocco.

"Is it signed?"

"Of course. It's one of seventy-five. Deluxe limited edition," Victor said.

"Nice."

Flint sat on the sofa and put her feet up on the coffee table, the feeling of anxiousness fading.

"What a lousy day."

"I heard about the murder up at the castle," Victor said. "How is Charles doing?"

"I'm not sure. He sputters a lot, but he's a hardy old man."

"I knew his family well. There's nobody left for him."

"Yeah…"

"There's something else on your mind."

"One of the witnesses may have seen Neil coming out of the study about the right time."

"I take it that's where Harris was found," Victor said.

"Yup."

"Don't jump to conclusions. You know where that can lead."

"I know. The witness hasn't verified who she saw yet. It could be mistaken identity," Flint said. She knew her father was right, but she worried anyway.

"I think I'll head off to bed," Victor said.

"Sure, Dad."

He pushed a lock of hair off her face and kissed her forehead.

Flint listened to the soft footfalls as he climbed the stairs. She heaved herself off the comfy sofa, headed back to the kitchen and wolfed down the lasagne her mom had left in the oven for her.

"I'm ready. Let's go." Flint put on a jacket and picked up the dog's leash.

Bodhi stood up and stretched, front legs out, head down. Down dog.

Flint caught the smell of salt air before she heard the lapping of the waves against the rocks below. The beam of her flashlight played across the lawn as she swept it back and forth. She took the path along the top of the outcrop to the old rustic steps that lead down to the water. Along the way, she lit up a cigarette, the first and only for the day. She palmed the lighter before sticking it back into her pocket. One day she would have to stop this, she thought. But not today.

Bodhi pounded down the stairs and waited for the okay to run wild. Flint sat on a deeply weathered step, taking her time. The dog vibrated. With a subtle wave of her hand, he shot off down the beach.

Flint tried not to think about Neil, but she couldn't stop the negative thoughts from creeping in. What if? Dangerous words to play with. She lit up another cigarette, against her rules, but the images bombarded her like watching a train wreck in slow motion. No survivors.

Before Flint did something stupid, like ignore a witness, she sent Hay a text to give him a heads-up about Kim and what she had said. He replied immediately that he had received her message. She knew he was probably having a cigar and cognac on his back porch, autumn chill or not.

Flint threw down the half-smoked cigarette, crushing it with her boot and climbed the steps.

Bodhi blasted by, giving her a gentle bump as he passed. Flint hurried home.

The circle of light thrown by the flashlight kept away the darkness of the night but not the darkness of her thoughts.

Chapter 7

The RCMP station was a plain, squat building on a side street behind the movie theatre. The south entrance with its large double oak doors gave access to the main detachment of four constables, one of whom was a community constable, and the supporting office staff. Flint's team had their own entry and parking spaces at the north end of the building.

The sergeant's office was filled with the normal stuff one would expect from the head of a major crime unit, filing cabinets, bookcases and a huge black glass-topped desk. But the individual touches the sergeant added transformed the space into a welcoming retreat. Rugs scattered across the grey floors were colourful and warm. There were several overstuffed chairs and a sectional sofa, comfy places to sink into, to decompress. Many late nights had found the detectives immersed deep into a case, sunk into the cushions, conversation rising and falling like the powerful ocean waves just twenty metres away.

Flint had gotten up before dawn to get a head start on her incident report. But mostly it was because she couldn't sleep with Neil's possible involvement in the murder making her mind work overtime. She sat in her leather chair, tapping away on the keyboard, occasionally glancing up from the computer screen to look at the framed photo of her little girl that she had placed on the corner of her desk.

Unaware of the time flying by, Flint kept her head bent down until she heard the clock strike another hour – six o'clock. She stared out the window, but only saw her reflection staring back. With a sigh she continued on, saving her work to the digital file that would go to the Nanaimo headquarters.

Flint also kept the complete paper trail of the investigation in a physical murder book. All the follow-up reports, crime scene photos, autopsy and forensic reports, witness interviews and notes would fill the book for future perusal by any number of detectives. If the case didn't get solved, the book would be a useful tool for reviewing key reports. Most departments had dismissed this old-fashioned collection of facts, but she still believed in its value. With the final sheet inserted in the book, Flint sat back in her chair. The tiniest bit of brightness announced the beginning of a new day. She looked out in the distance. Finally the sun rose, lighting the sky, not a cloud anywhere to mar the perfect clear blue.

* * *

Paulie had been up all night, searching for the door that the key would unlock. He had gone through most of the rooms, empty now before the rush of guests that would soon arrive and thwart his plans. Hurrying down the corridors, he opened each room and did a thorough look around. Time was running out.

* * *

The banging of the entry door, a clatter of boots, the chatter of voices and the entire team descended en masse into Flint's office.

"Whoa! The boardroom," the sergeant piped up, waving them out.

The group trooped down the hallway and ensconced themselves into their regular places around the long table.

Flint entered five minutes later, the murder book tucked under her arm. She looked toward the castle and sighed, then sat down with a thud.

Greenwood had her notebook opened to her last entry, ready with pen in hand, eager to learn. Thornberry stood in front of the white laminate counter, measuring out scoops of coffee for a fresh pot. Her hair fell in ringlets about her perfect skin. And the old-timer Constable Hay sat back in his chair, unaffected by the circumstances because of his many years working major crimes. His motto was *bring it on.*

An incident board had already been set up against the far wall, its glaring shiny surface blank except for a photograph of Harris Crest.

Flint leaned forward, placing her elbows on the tabletop and clasped her hands together.

"Okay. We have a busy day ahead of us. Thornberry. I want you to conduct the interviews with the attendees at the ceremony." She pushed a sheet of paper with the list of names across the smooth surface.

Thornberry glanced down at the list. "Holy shit. That's more people than I thought."

"Get a couple of the uniforms to give you a hand," Flint said. "Use one of their interview rooms." She turned to Hay. "You'll get the list of staff this morning?"

"You bet," Hay said.

"Send that over to Thornberry," Flint said.

"Really?" the corporal asked.

"You know the drill. We're all going to be pushed to the limit to get this done," Flint said. "The superintendent wants this solved. Pronto."

"Okay. Sorry." The corporal pushed back her chair. "I better get going." She rushed out the door and headed down the hallway.

"Now, Hay, leave the secateurs to me. I have a better job for you," Flint said. "If we could find the offending knife, we could put this case to rest." She held up her hand. "I know. I know. Like a needle in a haystack. But I've heard you are good at finding things in garbage bins." She snickered because that is exactly what happened in the case they had wrapped up in the summer. It was a small wonder she could find some humour in the middle of this disaster.

Hay shook his head. "So now you want me to go through the rubbish?"

"Well, if you think that would help. But seriously, I want you to check anywhere you didn't look yesterday. The parking lot. Inside the building."

"What's going on?" Hay asked.

"Well, let's just say I'm not convinced the runner was the killer. So let's make sure and look things over more thoroughly."

"You bet, boss," Hay said. "I'll get a couple of guys to help. If that is okay with you?"

"Absolutely," Flint said. "The early days are the most important so off you go."

"What about the witness? Did you still want me to pick up Kim to look at the photo?" Hay asked.

"Oh, shit I forgot about that," Flint said, although she had only put it on the back burner, out of sight, out of mind. But there was no getting around it, just another thing in her life that she would have to face up to. "Get it done."

"I'll go to the newspaper and ask the office manager to help find the article," Hay said. "She's an old friend of the family."

Flint nodded.

"Don't worry. It won't come to anything, I'm sure," Hay said. He pushed back his chair and hurried out.

After his departure, an odd sort of silence filled the room as Flint tried to figure out why she felt so despondent. There was no way it was Neil that Kim saw, she thought. It was times like these that she craved a cigarette. She looked up at the constable staring intently at her from across the table.

"What about me?" Greenwood asked, her brown eyes wide with anticipation.

"You stick close to me. To get the hang of how things work," Flint said.

The constable's eyes lit up. "All right."

"First things first. We'll head over to the castle and find out who owns these pruners," Flint said as she fingered the evidence bag. "Let's go."

They walked down the hallway making idle chatter, mostly about unimportant things. But Flint had something on her mind. She had to think of a way to ease the constable into the unpleasant task slated for later in the day, knowing it was an unavoidable undertaking that every detective had to face sooner or later.

"Dr. Churchman has scheduled an autopsy for this afternoon," Flint said, daring to glance over to Greenwood. "It's usual protocol."

"Oh, neat."

Flint smiled. The constable had that youthful countercultural look with the spiky hair, but she was no punk snot-nosed kid. She had guts.

This time when the sergeant pulled into the portico at the castle, there were several vehicles and a chartered bus jammed into the covered space. The unloading process was a three-ring circus with people and luggage everywhere. The atmosphere was one of gaiety and adventure, the guests being unaware of the tragic death that had occurred only yesterday. Flint was sure the news would spread quickly by the time happy hour rolled around.

After parking, the detectives made their way into the foyer. Flint stopped momentarily to admire the magnificence of the grand entrance.

"Unbelievable workmanship," Flint said. She glanced around. "There's the man we're looking for."

They made their way slowly past the piles of knapsacks and bags and people milling about, chatting and laughing.

"He's getting away," Flint said as the manager turned on his heels, not appearing to have seen the detectives.

Flint picked up her pace, shoving with her elbows as she struggled to catch up. "Mr. Webb," she shouted.

The elevator doors slid open.

"Hey, Paulie," Flint yelled.

Paulie stepped into the elevator.

Flint stuck her fingers in her mouth and ripped a whistle so loud everybody stopped. Heads turned toward the sound. Then, when there was no clear indication of trouble, things went back to normal. The chatter resumed, and the buzz continued.

Greenwood covered her ear too late. She had been standing next to the sergeant, and now the hollow ringing was like a bee circling round and round. It took a few attempts of opening and closing her mouth to make her eardrum pop.

Paulie had stopped in his tracks as well. He looked over, jamming his palm in the closing door and stepped out. "Detective. Sorry, I didn't see you." His face was pale, his eyelids droopy.

Flint nodded. "May we have a word with you?"

"Certainly. Let's go to my office," Paulie said. He pushed his hands into his pockets.

Flint sat on the hard chair, eying the manager. He was trying to avoid us, she thought. What the hell is he up to?

"I figured you would know who these belong to," she said as she laid down the pruners and pointed to the initials. "JJ."

Paulie snorted. "I see. That will be Janice Jenkins. She's an apprentice gardener, just out of high school."

"Is there a problem?"

"Well, she's quite a good worker, but I have an issue with her hanging around with the local kids on her breaks. I've had to mention it to her several times now."

Flint nodded.

"What's going on?" He fingered the evidence bag and looked up at the sergeant.

"Oh, nothing important. We just need to have a word with Janice," Flint said. "Would she be at the garden shed or somewhere on the grounds?" She looked at her watch. "Is it coffee time?"

"Let me call down there," Paulie said. He let it ring for quite a while before he hung up. "Nobody answered. Maybe she's with those kids again by the woods." He frowned and waved his hand in the air. "You can try your luck at the shed. If you go out the back entrance, it's past the clinic and then straight down the hill. You can't miss it." He leaned back into his chair and crossed his arms.

"Thank you," Flint said as she stood up to leave.

The detectives walked past the kitchen, the clinic and several closed doors. Flint peeked into a lunchroom on the left just before the back exit. A few people sat on long benches, staring into their coffee mugs, a sombre group. It would be a tough few days or weeks, if ever, before they would feel comfortable at their place of employment. She wondered how many would quit, rather than stick with it. Murder had a habit of stirring up emotions and scaring people away.

Thin wisps of smoke curled out of the shed's chimney and hung in the trees, giving the forest an ethereal atmosphere. Almost as if elves would pop out from behind the gnarly trunks and fairies would dance in the treetops.

Today it felt magical to Flint. Not cloaked in a menacing threat like last night when her fear of the dark had taken over.

There was a building behind the shed with an array of ride-on mowers standing idly on the concrete floor. Flint peeked inside, but there wasn't anybody around.

They strolled over to the garden shed. Flint knocked on the door.

"It's open," someone yelled out.

They entered a room with a pot-belly stove pumping out enormous amounts of heat. A plump girl sat at a picnic table. She put down the sandwich she was eating and pushed it away.

"We're not hiring."

"We're not here to find work. We're looking for Janice Jenkins," Flint said. "Is that you?"

"Yeah." She took a sip of her drink. "Who are you?"

"We're investigating Harris's death." Flint flipped open her badge.

Greenwood opened her wallet to show a new and untarnished shield.

"Oh." Janice chewed the inside of her cheek.

"We would like to ask you a few questions." Flint sat down across from the girl and placed the evidence bag on the table with the initials on the handle showing clearly through the plastic. "Are these yours?"

"Yeah, I wondered where they were. Thanks." She reached for the bag.

"Sorry, but I have to hang onto these for the time being." Flint laid her hand over the pruners.

"Really? But they're mine."

"They're evidence."

"For what? I didn't do anything." Janice sank back into her chair and pulled a long face.

"So you lost them yesterday morning?"

"Yeah, I told you that already."

Flint gave a little smile. The girl hadn't really said when she had lost them until now. "We found them in the garden bed by the study."

"Oh." Janice shrugged.

"Did you hear anybody talking with Harris?"

"No, I wouldn't. I always have my earbuds in," Janice said. She yanked at the wire hanging from her shoulder. "My music."

"Did you look in the window? See anybody?"

"No."

"So you didn't see or hear anything?"

"No."

"Okay. If anything comes to mind, give me a shout." Flint pushed a card across the table.

"Yeah, sure." Janice looked away.

Flint gestured to the constable with a tilt of her head. They stood up and left.

"She was real helpful," Greenwood said sarcastically as they stood outside the shed.

Before Flint could reply, her cell phone pinged. "It's Hay. Maybe he has some good news for us."

"You're not going to like this." Hay's voice boomed down the line loud enough that even Greenwood heard what he had to say.

But only Flint knew what he meant. She drew her hand through her hair, dreading what she was about to hear.

Chapter 8

"Wait. Where are you?" Flint asked. After a minute, she hung up. "He's here. We'll meet him in five."

Flint and Greenwood rushed up the hill and entered the interview room. Hay sat with a folder in front of him, a coffee in his hand and a tray of sandwiches on the table. They took seats across from him.

"It took us a while to locate the photo in question," Hay said. "My friend made the print as large as she could without losing too much detail." He pushed the photo over to the sergeant.

It was a glossy print in black and white. The photo had clearly been taken in the mayor's office. Flint could see the official town seal on the wall behind the men. Neil was the only council member who was dressed in a suit and tie. Charles stood beside a tall man with a hard hat tucked under his arm.

"That must be the real estate developer," Flint said.

"Bryson Williams," Hay said.

"This copy is quite grainy and it's overexposed," Flint said. "Is that as good as it gets?"

"I'm afraid so."

"So Kim picked out Neil from this photo?"

"Yeah, she did."

"How reliable is this girl as a witness?" Flint asked.

"We all know eyewitnesses are often more wrong than right," Hay said.

"Was Neil coming out of the study? Did she say?" Flint ran her finger along the edge of the photo.

"She was vague on that point."

"Okay. So the bottom line is she may have seen him in the foyer. That doesn't really mean much without some other evidence."

"You're right."

"Look, I forgot Thornberry was there. She saw Neil by the podium. Why don't you catch up with her and pin her down on a timeline. That would clear up this matter quickly."

"On it," Hay said. He shoved the photo in the murder book, rapped his knuckles on the table and left.

Greenwood sat quietly in her chair, taking it all in.

"May as well go to the morgue now. We'll stop off for a bite to eat after," Flint said as she stood up to leave. She didn't need these kind of complications, she thought. It was that old where there's smoke, there's fire thing, and she didn't like it. Not one bit.

"That sounds good."

The Hotel Dieu Hospital was quite a distance away on the outskirts of town. Traffic was horrible on the main roads at midday, but Flint knew all the back roads. She slipped easily through the suburbs, the neat and tiny houses thinning out as they hit the rural countryside. Travelling east along Woodruff Street there were few vehicles on the road, so she managed to get to their destination fairly quickly.

Flint turned at the newly erected entrance signage and drove down a tree-lined lane with grassy meadows beyond. The three-storey red brick building, standing back from the main road, came into view at the last curve. She skirted the large parking lot out front and made her way to the back. A flashy sports car with several official decals on the windshield belonged to the pathologist. Flint pulled into a space marked 'reserved' under a maple tree with sprawling limbs and no leaves. Its clean lines against the intense blue sky evoked the starkness of the northern landscape of late autumn days.

The detectives walked along the sidewalk to the morgue situated on the ground floor. All of the shrubs and flowers that had been flourishing in the summer were gone, leaving bare garden beds of rich, dark soil. The compost had the earthy aroma of a forest floor.

The steel door opened into a wide corridor, brightly lit by overhead florescent lamps. They followed the arrows to the end, passing several offices along the way. At the entry to the morgue Flint stopped.

"Are you ready for this?"

"So far," Greenwood said.

Flint tapped on the door before heading in. The chemical smell was not as strong as it had been the last time she was here. The grey walls had been painted with a fresh coat of white, and the floors had shiny new linoleum in a soft shade of blue. But there was no mistaking where they were. Couldn't get away from it. It was a cold sterile environment of an autopsy room. The taste of metal invaded their mouths almost immediately. Still, it was a great improvement over the previous décor.

"Hi, there," Dr. Kelly Churchman said. "How do you like it?"

"Way better," Flint said. She introduced Constable Greenwood to the pathologist and chit-chatted a few minutes about their families and the weather.

"All right. Let's get down to business," Churchman said. "There are no surprises." She pulled on a large handle and slid out a stainless-steel gurney with the victim laid out under a white sheet.

Flint glanced sideways at the constable, but Greenwood stood tall seemingly unaffected.

"First the head wound." With a few precise flicks of her wrist, Churchman rearranged the sheet so it draped down to Harris's waist. She tilted his head to the side and pointed to the large gash. "The wound is extensive. The skull is fractured in two places from hitting the hearth. That was the cause of death."

Greenwood had taken a position across from the pathologist, so she could see better. Flint was just glad that she was still standing.

"So let's move on to the cuts on his arms and hands." Churchman lifted the right arm. "It's like I said in the study. The victim raised his arms to fend off a knife attack. This was not an accident where the victim stumbled backward on his own. He was defending himself." She pulled the sheet back over his head. "Open and shut."

"And the time of death?"

"Within a few hours of when I examined him," Churchman said. "Sometime between nine and twelve."

"Okay, that lines up with our findings," Flint said.

"Is someone coming to identify the body?" the pathologist asked.

"There's really no need. Charles Crest was at the crime scene," Flint said. "I guess I have an obligation to ask him. But it's probably best that he doesn't come to the morgue. I'll get back to you on that."

"Okay," Churchman said.

"Thanks as always," Flint said.

The detectives headed outside, neither one of them talking. At the car Flint turned to the constable. "Well done."

"I used to hunt with my dad," Greenwood said. "Not quite the same, but you know what I mean."

"I suppose."

"My dad doesn't hunt anymore, so I don't either."

Flint looked at the constable, surprised at the things she said. Maybe it was just a thing to do with your dad. She thought back on the things she had done with her dad when she was a teenager. Boating. Hiking. Calm things.

They hopped in the vehicle and headed back into town. The Seabreeze Cafe was on the farthest end of Main Street where most of the bars and restaurants were located. After parking, they strolled down the sidewalk, remaining silent as they went.

Just ahead, they approached the gaping hole that separated the bank and the jewelry store. Shark Alley. Its towering brick walls stood two stories high, blocking out most of the sunlight on the sunniest of days. Flint picked up the pace as she walked past the entrance of the narrow alley, its gloominess looming large in her mind. She glanced at Altman's Jewelry and Diamonds storefront and hurried on to the cafe.

"Hey, wait up," Greenwood said, her attention momentarily distracted by a bright yellow deuce coupe across the street. She lagged behind the sergeant by several metres.

"Come on, then," Flint said.

Inside the cafe, the mood was a relaxing bustle with light-hearted laughter, mostly from the teenagers in the back booths. The older couples were ensconced at tables with checkered cloths while singles sat on chrome and vinyl stools at the long counter. The faded linoleum was worn and shiny from decades of customers coming and going.

Flint picked a stool near the cash register. Greenwood sat in the seat beside her.

"Hey, stranger," Paula Wilkes said as she poured two mugs of coffee.

The sergeant and the cafe owner were friends from high school. They had drifted apart when Flint had left town for work at the police unit in Kelowna. But after the shooting next door in the summer, they had reconnected.

"We have a murder up at the castle," Flint said. "Been kind of busy."

"I heard. Harris Crest, right?"

"Yeah."

"That's really a shame. Losing one kid is bad enough," Paula said.

"What's that you said?" Flint asked. "This is the second death?"

"Yeah, his older brother died." Paula paused. "I don't remember the details. It was a long time ago."

"Considering all that, Charles is holding up exceptionally well. He lost his wife, too."

"Yeah, poor man," Paula said and placed menus on the counter. "Do you want the special? It's a pasta dish."

"Sure."

Greenwood nodded her consent.

Paula removed the menus and placed their order. Within five minutes, she dropped off their lunch and left them to their thoughts as she hustled to refill coffee mugs and talk to the regulars.

The constable dug in while Flint sat quietly, pushing her food around with a fork, the chatter rising and falling in waves around them.

Flint had been avoiding coming into the cafe since the summer. It stirred up a lot of bad memories. How many times would it play in her head? Monthly, weekly, daily. The alley, the jewelry store, reminders of the romance with the fire chief heating up, then set ablaze by the unthinkable. A shooting, an arrest. Was it possible that it was happening all over again with Neil as a suspect? Was he a suspect?

Flint couldn't believe it. She stood up suddenly.

"Look I have some things to do. Head back to the station and write out your report for the day," Flint said. She tossed the vehicle keys on the counter and hurried out of the cafe.

Greenwood looked after her boss, knowing Flint was going rogue.

Chapter 9

City Hall was one street south of the cafe and a block over. The old building with its white stone accents and high arched windows was enclosed by a metre-high wrought iron fence. The gold and red leaves that carpeted the lawn had fallen from a large maple planted half a century before. Empty garden beds lined the curved sidewalk that led to the front entrance.

Flint hurried up the steps and entered an impressive lobby. The white walls contrasted with the black marble floors. Cove lighting accentuated the reception area with the seal of the town hung between Canadian and provincial flags.

The mayor's office was down the right corridor on the main level, but everyone had to sign in first, so Flint made a beeline to the dark-haired lady sitting behind the massive oak desk.

"Hi, Marlowe."

"Hello. Is Neil in his office?"

"No, I'm afraid you just missed him," the receptionist said. "He left an hour ago for a seminar in Victoria."

"Oh."

"It was a last-minute thing," she said. "One of your constables called in for him earlier. He said he would call again tomorrow. Is there something going on that I should know about?"

"No, not at all. When will Neil be back?" Flint asked, wondering why the mayor had left town without saying anything. It was unusual and made her worry even more.

"Let me take a look." She opened a drawer and flipped through a book. "He's staying overnight. Is your visit personal or business? Shall I book an appointment for you?"

"No. I was just dropping in to say hi," Flint said. She looked at the receptionist curiously. Was the woman trying to pry some information from her? "I'll give him a call on his cell. Thanks."

"No problem."

Flint stepped outside. Heavy clouds drifted across the darkening sky. A breeze had picked up, tossing the odd leaf across the grass and down the road. Thank goodness Neil wasn't in his office, she thought. Coming here to confront him had been a bad idea. She knew Hay would arrange to question him, as it should be. She stood on the walkway, trying to think of her next move. She glanced at her cell phone, but she hadn't missed any messages. It was getting late. The whole team had probably already left the station, sitting comfortably in front of blazing fires with their feet up or making dinner. She walked briskly toward her house as the streetlights came on. Then she broke into a jog and made it home in under twenty minutes, the shadows chasing in behind her. Darkness closed in early this time of year.

Flint bent over and placed her hands on her thighs and stayed there for a moment. She had been neglecting her routine running schedule and it showed. When she glanced up to her daughter's room, she saw the glow from a nightlight. She entered the back door, gave the dog a pat and hung up her jacket.

"Hi there. Are you hungry?" her mother, Oleane, asked. She picked up a washcloth and wiped the counter.

"I'm good, Mom. I had a late lunch." Flint sat at the table. "Well, maybe a cup of tea."

"I'll have one of those as well," Victor said. He pulled out a chair and settled in.

Flint felt her tense body relax and her shoulders drop as they chatted about all sorts of things, how well Paige was doing in kindergarten, the upcoming holidays, nothing heavy or serious. After an hour, her parents headed upstairs. It was a signal to the dog. Bodhi's ears twitched back and forth.

"Let's go."

Flint strolled down to the bottom of the lawn and sat on the wooden bench her father had built when she was a child. She lit up a cigarette and stared out into the ocean. The waves broke softly on the rocks in the shallows, their foamy crests swirling through the maze. The dog sniffed his way along the shoreline, stopping occasionally at a particularly interesting scent, then dashing off to the next smell.

The salty air and cool breeze on Flint's cheek made her sleepy. She headed back inside the house. Bodhi curled up into his bed as she switched off the light.

After looking into Paige's room to make sure all was as it should be, Flint changed into her pyjamas and sat on a cushion in the small window niche. The days were long during an investigation, so she rarely got home before her daughter's bedtime.

A razor thin crescent moon appeared high in the south western sky, its dim light barely cutting through the darkness. With little success of emptying her mind of the negative thoughts that had haunted her all day long, she gave up and went to bed. She tossed and turned most of the night, bombarded by her choices in life, not winning the battle to rein in her doubts.

* * *

Paulie perched on the edge of his bed and flung off his slippers. He slipped under the covers, the key on the night table crowding his thoughts. What the girl had told him about a treasure would be useless if he couldn't find the door that the key fit. He had searched the entire castle, pushing his way through the cobwebs and scaring mice back to their nests in the attic, exploring every nook and cranny in every room of the castle.

Suddenly it dawned on Paulie that he was looking in the wrong place. Maybe the answer was in one of the cottages. Maybe Harris's cottage. He tugged at the blanket, pulling it up to his chin and smiled. First thing in the morning. He had a plan.

Paulie closed his eyes and fell asleep, not even the rattling of the windows from the wind that had kicked up disturbing him.

Chapter 10

After another failed night of sleep, Flint left the house before anybody was awake. Although she supposed her father was lying in bed, listening to her movements, to the quiet closing of the back door and the start of the old Camaro thrumming in the stillness of the morning. She backed out of the garage and headed to the station. The sun rose slowly, filling the sky with pink and orange hues. She pulled up close to the front entrance surprised to see her police vehicle in the parking lot. That meant Greenwood was already here. She turned off the engine, knowing she would have to get a handle on her emotions.

Flint glanced in the offices as she made her way to the boardroom. Greenwood sat in her usual spot with the murder book in front of her. Her elbows were firmly planted on the table, head cradled in her hands, staring at a photograph. She jumped when the sergeant entered the room.

"What the hell are you doing here so early?" Greenwood asked. "How did you get here?"

"I drove," Flint said.

Greenwood leaned sideways, her face scrunched up.

"A 1969 Camaro," Flint said. "It's silver. It was my husband's."

"He let you have it?"

"Martin. He died."

"Sorry, I didn't mean to pry."

"It's okay. What are you up to there?" Flint asked.

"I was just reading over the reports from yesterday. To get a better feel of things."

"Any conclusions?"

"Not really. Just looking at the photograph from the newspaper."

Flint sat down beside the constable but didn't say anything.

Two sets of footsteps, heavy and hurried, could be heard coming toward the boardroom.

"Hey, guys," Thornberry said as she entered the room. She plopped herself down on the nearest chair.

"Boss," Hay said as he came in right behind her and sat down.

"Hay told me about the witness. She's full of shit. Neil never left the podium area, so there's no way she saw him in the foyer," Thornberry said.

"Well, that's definitive," Flint said. She smirked at how the corporal didn't mince words.

"She should have kept her mouth shut if she wasn't sure. That's how people get into trouble."

"Mmmm." Flint felt a huge sense of relief.

"I noticed that Bryson has the same curly hair as Neil. That's what I was looking at," Greenwood spoke up. "Maybe he's the guy she saw?"

"Harris had an issue with Bryson over the property line," Hay said.

"Has anybody had a chat with Bryson yet?" Flint asked.

"I tried to get a hold of him yesterday, but he didn't answer, and his voice mailbox was full. I'll have another go today," Hay said.

"Yeah, get on that. So the property has been thoroughly searched?"

"Just about. I want to take another look down by the shoreline. If that's okay with you."

"It's probably a lost cause but go ahead. Be thorough," Flint said.

"Absolutely," Hay said.

"I'm working down the list of people who attended the ceremony," Thornberry said. "I'm not having any luck. No one noticed anything. Same with the staff. It's a dead end. But I'll keep on going with it."

"Okay. Let's get cracking," Flint said. "Greenwood. You're with me. We'll have a chat with Bryson."

The team split up, each on a mission. Although with a lack of evidence or any real suspect, it seemed a daunting task.

"Whoa! Nice car," Greenwood said as she stepped outside.

The Camaro was low to the ground with a mean-looking front end.

"Thanks. I don't take it out that much," Flint said. "Especially in the wet weather." She looked up to the sky where thunderous clouds had gathered over the past few hours. A storm off the Pacific Ocean was brewing. It would come in waves with a deluge of rain and high winds. "Sometimes I get caught."

The constable smiled. "Still, can we take your vehicle?"

"Sure. Why not?"

Flint started up the car, its engine roared to life then settled into a steady purr.

Greenwood sat back in the luxurious leather.

The tires squealed as the sergeant pulled out of the station. "Sorry," Flint said, but she wasn't. It felt good. Before they had reached the end of the street, her cell phone pinged. It was the pathologist. She spoke for a few minutes before hanging up.

"Dr. Churchman said she can release the body by tomorrow," Flint said. "I guess we better pay Charles a visit first. Sort that out and see how he's doing at the same time. It's closer anyway."

"Fine with me," Greenwood said.

Flint headed up the long road to the castle. As they approached the building, there were several signs indicating the way to the parking area. Pine needles knocked down by the latest windstorm covered the ground with a crunchy, thin layer. She took a quick look around the half-empty lot in search of a secluded spot where her car wouldn't get dinged.

Flint turned off the engine and a quietness descended upon them, broken only by the shrieks of seagulls circling over the treetops.

They walked along a gravel path to the front of the building, past the fountain and headed down the long expanse of lawn to the cottages. As they came over the ridge, Greenwood saw a tall man scurrying across the clearing into a patch of trees, his hair caught in the updraft of wind blowing in from the west. He was dressed in corduroys and a heavy knitted sweater, looking like he belonged in the countryside.

"Hey, isn't that Bryson?" Greenwood asked.

Flint's attention was directed to the large waves crashing on the shore behind the cottages. She turned to the constable. "What?"

"I think that man was Bryson."

"I didn't see anybody," Flint said.

"He just went through there." Greenwood pointed to the woods.

"We'll take a look when we're finished here. There used to be a deserted shack on the beach. Maybe he's using it for his headquarters," Flint said. She knocked on the door of Charles's cottage.

"Come in."

They stepped inside. "May we sit?"

"Sure."

They sat down in the chairs in front of the fireplace. The fire crackled and hissed from a newly laid piece of fir, making the room feel like a sauna. Soft music from a radio played in the background. The warmth immediately made Flint feel overheated. She undid the buttons on her jacket.

"The pathologist will release the body soon," Flint said. "So you can arrange for a funeral now."

The old man faltered slightly at her words, hunching his shoulders as he swiped the moisture from his eyes.

"We're sorry for your loss," Flint said. She wasn't sure what to say or do. He had been holding up strong the other day.

A glass of an amber liquid, maybe whisky, was on the table beside him. He reached for it and took a huge swig.

"Was that Bryson who was just here?" Greenwood asked as she gazed at an empty glass on the coffee table.

Flint glanced at her sideways and frowned.

"He visits me quite a lot." Charles looked over to the constable.

"Is he related to you?" Flint's eyebrows shot up.

"No. No. He's just a friend," Charles said. "We have a drink and talk about the old days."

Flint sat back in her chair, trying to figure out the dynamics of the relationship. She was fairly certain that Bryson was no friend of Harris. Or was that just the manager's take on it?

"Were Harris and Bryson friends?"

Charles sighed loudly before he answered. "Once upon a time they were. But lately, they seemed to be at odds with each other."

"Was there something specific that happened?"

"Maybe it was the development Bryson was planning next door. He's putting in a row of private beachfront cabins. I overheard them arguing about it one day a few weeks ago. Harris confronted him about it. Said he didn't like it. Look, don't get me wrong. It was a disagreement not a fist fight. They just didn't see eye to eye about the whole thing." The old man stopped as if he was trying to decide how much to say. "My son changed over the years. He had a habit of pushing people's buttons. Always trying to get the upper hand on business deals and..."

Flint remained silent to let him finish his thoughts.

"I guess that's not a nice thing to say about one's own flesh and blood, but it's the truth." Charles eyed the sergeant warily. "But no matter. Whoever did this, Harris didn't deserve to die like that." The old man didn't stop the flow of tears that ran down his cheeks, catching on his chin and dripping onto his shirt.

"Do you think it was an ongoing quarrel or did they drop it?" Flint asked, hoping she wasn't pushing him too far.

"I can't talk about it anymore." He grabbed the glass and gulped the last of his drink, some of it dribbling down the side of his mouth.

"Sorry. We'll go now." Flint gestured with a tilt of her head toward Greenwood and stood up. "Take care."

The detectives stepped outside and stood on the stoop.

"Holy shit," Greenwood said, her brown eyes wide with surprise. "Did he just implicate Bryson? That sure sounded like a motive for murder."

"Let me think." Flint was stunned at the old man's candor. She tried to sort out the conversation in her mind. What had Charles really said? He had been upfront that Bryson and Harris had argued a few weeks ago. But when asked if they were still at each other, he had declined to answer. Had the men settled their difference? Or had the acrimony continued that morning in the study and ended with a push? A fatal push?

A brittle wind gusted through the trees and whipped around the cottage. Pine needles flew through the air like tiny darts.

Chapter 11

"I can't believe the old man just pointed a finger at his buddy," Greenwood continued.

"Hold on. Bryson is definitely a person of interest. That's all. We'll speak to him and sort out fact from fiction." Flint didn't want to jump to conclusions no matter how bad it looked. She had been caught in that tangled web before, things were not always what they seemed. This was a very high-profile case with high stakes for the community. The residents were already up in arms about how this could happen right under the noses of the police. Not to mention how the superintendent would feel if they got it wrong. It was a mess. But murder was always untidy.

Flint pushed the jumble of thoughts away and stepped off the porch. The cottage next door was dark, no inviting lights or smoke curling from the chimney. The police tape across the doorway fluttered in the wind.

"Hey, it looks like someone has broken into Harris's place," Flint said. She strolled over to take a better look. The lock on the door had been jimmied.

"What would they want? Did Ryan find something?" Greenwood asked as she came up behind the sergeant.

"I don't know. I haven't heard back from him yet," Flint said.

She pulled her cell out of her pocket and dialled the forensic scientist. It rang and rang, then went to voice mail. She left a message for him to get back to her as soon as possible.

"Should we go in?" Greenwood asked.

"No. The damage is already done. We'll wait until we hear from Ryan," Flint said. "Let's go for a walk."

They hustled down the path through the woods and came out onto a long stretch of meadow overlooking a sandy beach. Straight ahead, a small tin-roofed shack standing on a rise was taking the full force of the wind. A displeasing thin, metallic sound resonated with each gust.

A newly washed blue Bronco was parked at an angle under the lone fir tree. Although the building looked in good repair, the yard was in shambles. There were water-soaked cardboard boxes, rusty filing cabinets, empty wine bottles, broken chairs and old office furniture. A burn barrel with a steel gate on top stood on a concrete block. Beside it was a stack of rotten planks, some plywood and old roof shingles.

They walked up to the front entrance. Over the doorway, a small sign was screwed into place, announcing 'Bryson Beach Development'.

"Guess we're at the right place," Greenwood said. "Someone needs to tidy up though."

Flint knocked on the door and stepped back off the narrow stoop.

"Come in," someone yelled.

With little effort, the door opened outward. The room was small and crowded with boxes taking up most of the floor space. The walls were plastered with colourful photographs and illustrations, undoubtedly of the proposed development. At the back, a man behind a grey metal desk stood up and greeted them.

"Have a seat." He pointed to the folding chairs. "How can I help you?"

"Are you Bryson Williams?" Flint asked. Both detectives pulled out their badges.

"Yes." He looked from one to the other.

"We would like to have a word with you."

"Sure. No problem," Bryson said. "It's about Harris, I take it."

"Yes," Flint said before sitting down. "Were you at the ceremony next door?"

"No, I wasn't."

"You weren't curious about what was in the time capsule?"

"Not really," Bryson said.

"Oh, I see," Flint said.

"I'm not at this office very often. I haven't got it organized yet." He gestured around the room to the mess.

"Where were you the morning Harris was killed?"

"You don't think I had anything to do with that?"

Flint stared at the man.

"I was at home."

Flint pulled the photo from her pocket, unfolded it and laid it on the table. She turned it so Bryson could see. "Is this you?"

"Sure. That photo was taken at the mayor's office when I announced my project." He paused. "What's going on?"

"Just checking some details. Nothing to worry about," Flint said. "I understand you and Harris were friends."

"Maybe once upon a time. We've known each other for quite a while. If you want to know, I'm sorry about what happened to him."

"So you're not friends anymore?" Flint asked, wanting to pin down their relationship.

"I suppose not," Bryson said. "What are you getting at?"

"Did you force Harris to dig up the capsule because it was on your property?" Flint asked, ignoring his question.

"Who told you that? That's a lie. I wouldn't do that. Harris dug up the capsule on his own. I told him I wouldn't disturb it. Mostly for respect to his father."

"But you did have an argument with him about the development," Flint said.

"No. Well, somewhat," Bryson said. He stopped and considered his answer before continuing.

Flint could see him calculating how deep to step into it.

"Just the truth will work," she said.

Bryson rubbed at his chin before he spoke.

"Look, I wouldn't call it an argument. More like a disagreement. I bought this piece of land from Charles several years ago. It was just a few months ago that I decided to start my project. I needed to get my finances together. You know, the paperwork, the permits, the backers. Now that the time had come Harris made it clear to me that he objected. I tried to appease him, you know, show him the bright side of it. I wasn't going to stop just because he wanted me to. I have a lot of money riding on this."

"What was the bright side?" Flint asked as she narrowed her eyes.

"My development would bring in more people. There was a good chance guests would go up to the castle to eat," Bryson said. "It's a win-win situation. That's what I told him."

"Did you have more than one argument about it?"

"What? You mean, did I go to the study and end it all? That's absurd."

"Okay." Flint felt like she wasn't getting anywhere with her questioning and thought maybe it was useless to carry on. "Do you have any idea why Harris objected to your development so strongly?"

"Not really. That's just the kind of guy he was," Bryson said. "If he's not in charge of the situation, he's pissed off. I didn't have anything to do with what happened. I told you all I know. Now I would really like to get back to work."

Bryson leaned forward and shuffled a few papers around the desk.

"If you think of anything else." Flint placed her card down and stood up.

"Sure. I really am sorry about Harris. Charles is devastated by his death." Bryson paused. "Sorry, I didn't mean to be rude. It's just that I'm behind schedule."

"Thanks for your help," Flint said.

The door almost got away from the sergeant when she pushed on it, caught by a sudden strong rush of wind. She made sure it clicked before releasing her hold.

"Whoa! Big storm is almost here," Flint said.

"Do you think Bryson did it?"

"It doesn't matter what I think. We need evidence." As an afterthought, Flint said, "It's too early to rule him out though. Maybe at the top of the list."

They walked back through the woods to the castle.

"Should we get something to eat?" Greenwood asked. "It's late. I'm starving."

"Let's make it a sit-down for a change," Flint said.

The detectives went over the conversation they'd had with the real estate developer without coming to any conclusions. After lunch they headed to the parking lot. As soon as Flint started the engine, her cell phone pinged. She switched off the ignition and answered.

"Ryan, I hope you have something for us."

The sergeant hung up after only a few minutes, a widening frown on her face signalling no such luck.

"The only blood at the crime scene and on his clothes was from the victim himself," Flint said. "They didn't find anything at Harris's cottage, either. But he'll take another look."

"That's weird," Greenwood said. "Why the hell did someone break in then?"

"It could be kids," Flint said. "Although, I don't like it."

"Yeah."

"They're finished with the capsule and will be sending it over to us tomorrow," Flint said. "There were too many prints on it to single anyone out. The contents, as well. That's all we got."

Flint started up the car again and pulled away. She put her foot on the gas and zoomed down the long road to the station, taking the curves with less caution than usual.

Greenwood hung on but didn't say anything. She kind of liked it.

When they arrived at the parking lot, a text came in.

"Thornberry is finished with the interviews. Not one witness in the whole group. Unbelievable," Flint said. "I'll send a text to the rest of the team. Meeting first thing in the morning. Could you pick me up?"

"Sure."

Greenwood hopped out of the Camaro. She stared at the vehicle as Flint zipped down the street, round the corner and out of sight, the rumble of her muffler reverberating above the blustery south-west wind.

* * *

Paulie hadn't counted on Harris's cottage to be part of the investigation. The crime scene tape over the door had taken him by surprise. He was determined to get inside, tape or no tape. But he needed to be cautious with the police still swarming around the property. And that stupid gardener. She was always hanging around with her friends, even after hours. He wanted to fire her ass, but his hands were tied because she had been signed up for an apprenticeship before he was made manager.

After pushing away all the negative thoughts, he set to work. The tape gave away easily. Before entering, he took one last look around to make sure nobody had seen him. After a half an hour of poking around, looking for the matching lock to the key he held in his sweaty palm, he gave up. It was too small of a space to be hiding anything at all. Besides, at any moment, someone might intrude upon him, and then what could he say?

Paulie sat at his desk fuming. His plan was falling apart quickly. His next step was to find Mia. But she had called in sick and wasn't answering her phone. He tried again, letting it ring until the answering machine came on. There was no point in leaving a message. She would see his number on the display. But why after several rings and many hours later hadn't she returned his call? He thought about heading over to her place but then thought better of it. She could file a harassment suit against him, although he had thought they were friends. Maybe it had been a hoax played on him all along. What a fool he had been to believe some lowly waitress. He slammed the door as he left for home, pissed off at everyone.

* * *

The full force of the mighty ocean pounded mercilessly on the rugged coastline. Flint could hear the crashing of water as soon as she stepped out of her car. Above her, the giant fir trees that had stood in place for decades swayed and creaked with the heavy blasts of wind. The rain had just started. She knew by the morning the long, rolling waves left behind would provide surfing joy to those who dared ride the four metre beauties.

Flint petted the dog and headed upstairs to catch a glimpse of her daughter. She stood by Paige's door out of sight and listened to the murmur of her mother's soft voice as she read a tale from a favourite book. Recognition of the story from her own childhood brought a smile to her face. She would come back later to kiss Paige on her forehead, not wanting to disturb the peaceful scene between her mom and her daughter.

Flint went downstairs and stopped short of entering the living room where her dad sat in his chair. He turned when he heard the padding of feet and motioned her to sit.

"Neil has been calling here."

"I figured that."

"You didn't answer his calls?"

"I couldn't. I just couldn't deal with that right now. With everything that's happening..."

"You can't leave him hanging."

"I know. He's been ruled out anyway," Flint said.

"But?"

"I don't think I have to tell you how it feels. You get it."

"You've been through a lot," Victor said. "Give it some time. No rush to judgement."

"Thanks, Dad. I don't know what I'd do without you."

"I took the dog out earlier. He seemed antsy."

"I'll send him out the back on his own for a minute. It's way too rainy," Flint said.

"Good idea. Mom left some food in the oven."

Flint gave her dad a peck on the cheek and headed off to the kitchen. She let the dog outside and dug into a casserole that had been left for her, not realizing how hungry she was. Her mom came in after she finished her meal.

"Go see your daughter."

"Thanks for everything, Mom."

After hanging out with Paige for a half-hour, Flint headed back to the kitchen where a fresh pot of tea was brewing.

They talked for a while about normal things, a new pair of shoes for Paige, a recipe for lemon meringue pie her mom had gotten from a friend, how the dog was getting chubby. It felt good to belong, a sane and dependable family. Safe.

With the dog back in the house and after he shook every single drop of water onto the floor, Flint went up to her bedroom.

Flint lay in bed, listening to the downpour, thinking of the stormy relationships she had since the loss of her husband. Maybe it would be a good idea to tell Neil she just couldn't do it.

A crack of thunder made her sit up. She counted the number of seconds between the next flash and the thunder. It was far enough away not to worry. She pulled the blanket up to her chin, her eyelids feeling heavy. Finally she succumbed to sleep, even as the winds continued unabated, hammering against the house. Even as her troubled thoughts invaded her dreams.

Chapter 12

Flint woke up with a kink in her neck. She hopped into the shower, dressed, grabbed a coffee and headed outside before anyone in the household stirred. The sun was shining brightly, but there was a crispness to the air. She pulled her jacket in closer to her body, glad that she had donned a sweater underneath. All they had to look forward to over the next few months was colder and stormier days. Until at least March. But in spite of all this, actually because of this, she knew the surfers would be out in full force today, riding the waves, oblivious to the harsh weather, revelling in it. She thought about the surfers enough, maybe she should give it a try.

Flint walked down to the end of the driveway where Greenwood was sat in the police vehicle ready and waiting to pick her up. They arrived at the boardroom to find Thornberry and Hay bent over laptops, working on their reports.

Flint sat down, gave the team an update from Ryan and told them about the break-in at the cottage.

"Here's another thing. I picked this up yesterday at Bryson's office." The sergeant pulled a glossy brochure from her pocket and placed it on the table. "This is Bryson dressed up smartly in a suit and his hair combed neatly. Who does he remind you of?"

"He looks like Neil," Hay said.

"They could almost be brothers," Thornberry said, her eyes widened.

"That's what I thought," Flint said.

"I guess I should show it to Kim," Hay said. "He could be the man she saw."

"Get it done as soon as you can. Apparently, Bryson and Harris had issues with each other."

"You don't say."

"When you're done with Kim, give Thornberry a hand with the paperwork. We're getting bogged down."

"You bet," Hay said.

Flint's cell pinged. She read the text and turned to Greenwood.

"Ryan gave us the okay to go into Harris's cottage. He was there again early this morning. He agreed someone had broken in, tipped over a chair and riffled through some drawers. But besides that, nothing had changed."

"So it probably was just some kids," Greenwood said.

"I don't know what I think about it right now, but we're going to take a look regardless," Flint said. "Okay, everyone. Listen up. Let's get things done. We'll meet back here this afternoon."

Everyone nodded in agreement.

Hay picked up the phone and dialled Kim while the corporal hunkered down to bring the murder book up to date.

"See you guys later," Greenwood said and headed out the door with the sergeant.

She drove to the castle with Flint sitting quietly in the passenger seat. After parking in the first lot, they walked to the cottage in silence. The police tape lay in pieces about the yard, having been whipped around by the high winds.

Flint pushed aside the last of the tape and entered, the constable following in behind.

It was just as Ryan had said. Flint picked up the overturned chair and looked in the open drawers. She picked up a book from the coffee table and flipped through a few pages.

"Anything interesting?"

"Just some poetry," Flint said and replaced the book. "Somebody was in here looking for something, but I wonder what it was?"

"I don't know," Greenwood said.

Flint took a quick look in the other rooms and walked out of the cottage. "There's nothing here for us. Let's grab some lunch before we head back to the station."

"How about pizza? There's a new restaurant a friend of mine just opened up," Greenwood said, rushing to catch up with the sergeant. "They couldn't afford the rent on the main drag, so they're over two blocks. I hope they can make a go of it."

"Sure. Let's do it. We'll bring some back for the other guys."

The restaurant wasn't busy, so they got their order promptly and were soon back at the station. They hurried to the boardroom where the other detectives were busy working.

The polished steel cylinder gleamed in the room's bright light, not a mark or fingerprint blotting its smooth surface. The bolts on either end holding it together made it look futuristic, almost robotic-like. A pair of white gloves in a plastic bag lay on the table beside it.

"Holy crap, it's here," Greenwood said.

"Ryan just dropped it off," Hay said.

"When I saw it in the study, I was surprised. It's more substantial than I thought it would be," Flint said.

"That's what I thought, too," Thornberry said.

Flint put the pizza boxes down and opened the lids. The hefty smell of oregano and cheese filled the air. "Let's eat while it's hot."

She sat down and took a slice of the vegetarian pizza. Before her teeth sunk into the first bite, her cell phone pinged. She glanced at the screen and put the food back on the napkin.

"I have to take this." Flint got up and headed outside, closing the door behind her. After five minutes, she returned to the room. "That was the superintendent."

"What's up?" Hay asked.

"He just wanted an update."

"Okay."

"I told him how much we like having Greenwood on our team, as well."

"Really?" the constable said.

"Yeah. You're doing good."

Greenwood beamed.

Another ping sounded.

"I have to go."

"What's up?" Greenwood asked.

"Paige broke her arm." Flint grabbed her jacket. "Keep busy."

They heard the thud of the sergeant's boots fade away and then the bang of a door.

"What now?" Greenwood asked. "Should we open the capsule?"

Their eyes were drawn to the shiny container.

"No way," Hay said. "We have to wait until the boss is back."

"We have lots to do," Thornberry said. "No worries there."

"I'll give Kim another ring," Hay said. "Not that I don't want to hang out with you guys." He chuckled and left the room.

"Sure," Thornberry said.

"What about me?" Greenwood asked.

"You can help me with the paperwork."

"Oh."

"Get used to it," Thornberry said. "You're the junior officer here. Don't forget."

The constable rolled her eyes.

* * *

At the hospital, Flint found her dad sitting in a chair just inside the doorway with a book on his lap.

"She's fine. Don't panic," Victor said and patted the seat next to him. "Sit."

"What happened?"

"She got her leg stuck in the rocks and fell down. It's a simple break. Mom's with her. They should be out soon."

"Are you sure Paige is okay?" Flint asked. "She must be scared."

"Look. There they are now," her dad said.

Oleane and Paige walked down the corridor, hand in hand. The cast on her arm looked huge. But really it was the slightness of the young girl's body that made it appear so.

Flint glanced at her mother.

"She was a real brave girl," Oleane said and turned to her granddaughter. "Weren't you?"

"I'm okay. You're not mad at me, are you?"

"No, of course not. Let's get you home," Flint said and sighed heavily. "Do you want to ride in the big car with the lights on?"

"Yeah." Paige released her hand from her grandma's and skipped out the sliding doors with her mom.

When they got home, Paige was put to bed with cozy blankets tucked around her. Flint sat beside her and read her fairy tales until she fell asleep. Exhausted with emotion and stress, she closed the book and laid it on the bedside table, then slipped out of the room and headed downstairs. Her parents were in the kitchen, drinking tea and talking in hushed whispers.

"She's settled down now," Flint said.

"It happened so fast, I–" Oleane started.

"Mom, it's nobody's fault." Flint slung her arms around her mother's shoulder. "Paige is an active child. Don't worry." She released her hold. "I feel drained. I'm just going outside to get some air. That will make me feel better."

"Okay, sweetheart," Oleane said.

Her dad nodded sagely.

Flint stood on the lawn. She lit up a cigarette and inhaled deeply. A rustle of leaves made her turn toward the sound. She hadn't heard a vehicle pull into the driveway. It was Neil. She flung her smoke on the ground and crushed it with her boot.

Neil hopped out and walked toward her.

"Marlowe. Can we talk?" Neil asked. "I tried to call you."

Flint lowered her head and rubbed at her temple, a headache coming on strong. She didn't know if she could handle this, but she knew she couldn't avoid this conversation forever. May as well get it over with.

"I know. I meant to call back, but I've been super busy," Flint said, thinking that was mostly true. She kept her gaze toward the ground. "It's been a horrendous day."

"I bet." Neil paused. "I don't know why that girl said it was me she saw." He locked eyes with Flint. "But you know it wasn't. She made a mistake."

"I know that," Flint said. "It's been sorted."

"That's a relief," Neil said. "Are we good?"

"Let's talk in a few days," Flint said. "It's not a good time right now."

"Okay," Neil said. "I'll be there when you need me." He squeezed her arm and walked away.

Flint watched him as he got into his vehicle and drove away. She lit up another cigarette, took two hits and headed back inside. Did she have room in her heart for him? For any man? Why did everything come at her at the same time? Was it the same for everyone? She supposed it was. Like bad things come in threes. What number was she working on? Two, she thought.

Chapter 13

Flint felt the warmth of the sun on her face before she opened her eyes. She heard the steady, soft breathing of Paige next to her. A cry in the night had woke her up. It had been a long night of fitful sleep. Her head throbbed and her arm was numb from being wrapped around her daughter. She glanced over; the baby quilt that had survived countless crises was tangled in the tiny limbs, a stuffed bunny by her head.

Flint carefully rolled onto her side and slipped from the bed. She closed the door behind her and headed to her own room. After a shower, she still felt not of this world, a tiredness had taken a hold of her – body and soul. She tiptoed downstairs and sat in the kitchen alone, listening to the birds awakening outside. The dog lay in his bed, smart enough to know not to disturb the household quite yet.

"Shh," Flint said, finger to lips. She opened the door and headed to the edge of the property while Bodhi trotted off in a different direction. After glancing back toward the house, she lit a cigarette. A light shining in the living room window told her that her dad was up. She was grateful he had left her to her own devices. He knew her as well as any of the novels he had lining his bookcase.

It wasn't often that Flint let herself have a smoke so early in the day, but she felt her life had been turned upside down. It was bad enough that she had to deal with the complexity of a murder case, but the personal involvement as brief as it was, had thrown her for a loop. On top of it all, she had an injured child on her hands. A reminder of how tenuous life really was. Then she realized that was the third bad thing. Hopefully that was the end of it.

Flint crushed out her cigarette, having determined to take the day off. She would work from home. Family first, be damned. She sat on a smooth piece of driftwood and gazed out to the rolling ocean. After looking at her watch, she pulled out her cell phone and dialled the corporal.

Thornberry answered on the first ring.

After a short chat explaining what she was doing, Flint told her the capsule would have to wait until she was back in the office the following day. She heard the disappointment in Thornberry's voice and felt a pang of guilt, but only for a nanosecond.

Bodhi reappeared and the two of them headed back inside. When Flint opened the back door, the sweet smell of coffee and smoked bacon flooded her senses. Comfort food.

"We're having pancakes. My favourite," Paige said. She sat in a grownup chair, her chin touching the edge of the table, refusing to be propped up with pillows or a booster seat.

It seemed as if the cast on her daughter's arm was barely in the young child's thoughts, if at all. Flint smiled and sat down next to her dad.

"Isn't this nice. Are you staying for a while?" Victor asked.

"I'm going to work from home today."

"I've got the fire going already."

"How do you always know what I'm going to do before I even know?"

"He's psychic," her mother said, placing a coffee on the table for her.

After breakfast, Flint settled down in the living room while her mom and daughter took a short stroll with the dog. Her phone pinged. She scanned the screen and answered. Not expecting any great revelations, figuring it was just Thornberry being Thornberry. Always up for a chat. But she was wrong.

"All right," Flint shouted, then put her hand over her mouth.

Victor glanced up from his book.

After she got off the phone, she sat back into the cushions.

"Well, we finally got a lead. That waitress, Kim, who had originally picked out Neil has changed her mind. Now she swears it was Bryson who bumped into her by the study."

"That's good," her dad said and buried his head back into his novel.

"Yeah."

Except how many times will the girl change her mind, Flint thought. And as urgent as it was to speak to Bryson, the man seemed not to feel the same. Hay had tried several times to phone, but Bryson had neither answered nor returned his calls. Suspicious behaviour for someone who said he was innocent. His wife was just as evasive when Hay spoke to her. Apparently, she had no idea where he was or when he was returning. She said it wasn't her business to keep track of her husband. Oh, really.

But thinking on it, what did they really have? An argument that Bryson said was a disagreement, a falling out of friends. And didn't that happen all the time? And a wishy-washy witness. No physical evidence to link the man to the crime. So basically all they had were rumours and suspicions.

Flint dialled the superintendent, but he was in a meeting so she left a message.

Victor got up and shoved another log on the fire and sat back down.

"Neil just got caught in the crossfire. You shouldn't lay blame at his feet," Victor said and looked at his daughter. "He's a good man."

"I'll sort it out. Don't worry," Flint said. She yawned, stretching her arms over her head. "Did you know Harris's mother?"

"Yes. She was a beautiful-looking woman. A real social butterfly when she was young. She wore long skirts and wrote poetry. I'm not sure how she ended up with old man Crest."

"Well, he wasn't old when they met, I'm sure."

"No. But Charles was always kind of a stick-in-the-mud guy," Victor said. He laughed, then turned serious. "There was a—"

"Mommy," Paige screamed as she tumbled into the room. "We had a super walk."

"I'm sure you did, sweetheart," Flint said. "Is it time to settle down for a bit?" She patted the cushion beside her. "Come sit with me."

"Okay." Paige rested her head on her mother's lap and immediately fell asleep.

"The doctor prescribed some medication. He said it would make her sleepy," Oleane said. "I'll take her upstairs."

"Thanks," Flint said and stuck her nose into her notes.

At lunchtime, the family gathered around the kitchen table and enjoyed some homemade soup. Afterwards Flint went to her office and shut the door. It was the only way to get any work done. There were too many distractions in the living room.

As the light in the room faded, Flint looked outside at the darkening sky. She wondered why Thornberry hadn't called again. Because there wasn't any news was her best and only guess. Where to go next with the investigation? Her notes were concise but gave her no direction. Her cell phone pinged. Finally, maybe something happened. The text was from Thornberry. Another ping, another message.

The first message said they were caught up on the reports. The second one said they had closed up shop and gone home. Flint put her files on the desk and stood up. Well, that was that, she thought.

"Coffee time," Flint said and headed to the kitchen. She grabbed a mug, sat down and looked toward the ocean. Paige and her dad were sitting on the bench by the water. The dog stood in front of a large tree staring at a squirrel with a nut in his mouth.

"Did you get any work done?" her mom asked and sat down opposite her.

"Not really. Just reading over everything," Flint said. "Sometimes something you hadn't noticed before pops out at you."

"Will you be working late tomorrow?" Oleane asked.

"It's hard to say. Depends. What's on your mind?" Flint refilled her mug.

"It's the Christmas light up at the castle," Oleane said. "I thought we could have dinner and watch."

"I forgot. It seems to get earlier each year," Flint said.

"It's always the last week in November," Oleane said. "So what do you think?"

"Sure. I think Paige is old enough now to enjoy that."

"Perfect. Done."

"What do you mean done?"

"I already made reservations for us. Window seat for the VIPs."

"Right." Flint laughed. Something besides doom and gloom.

* * *

Paulie was fuming. He had the key to a door that he couldn't find, to a treasure that would be all his. Mia had come back to work, but she was avoiding his questions. She said she didn't know what the key unlocked, only that

Harris had told her it was the greatest gift of all. Whatever the hell that meant? Gold bars, coins? He fingered the key again, so close but so far away.

What was her game anyway? Did Mia want a cut? Yeah, he was sure of it. She was holding back on information, pissed off that he had gained possession of the key.

He had a hard time concentrating on his work. Tomorrow was the light up, and he hadn't even checked to see if everything was ready. Damn.

* * *

The ambulance ground to a halt under the portico. Two men sprang out, pulled a stretcher from the back and dashed down the hill to the cottages. They hoisted the old man into the vehicle, strapping him in. A paramedic gave him oxygen, worried about his raspy breathing. The sirens screamed and the lights flashed as the ambulance headed down the long winding road. Charles reached his hand out to the man looking down at him and passed out.

Chapter 14

The air was crisp when Flint stepped outside and walked down the driveway to her vehicle. There was just a smidgeon of grey on the edges of the blue sky, a few stars still twinkling near the western horizon. In an hour, the depth of the blue would be in stark contrast to the black sea. Overhead, the sound of honking made her look up. A late migrating flock of Canada geese flew in a V-formation, southbound to their winter feeding grounds. Lovely to see, but a sign of the changing seasons.

Flint pulled up to the station and sat for a minute to quell the unease she had been feeling for days. This was only the second murder case where she had been the lead detective. It was a bit unnerving to be the person in charge. The first case had been solved fairly quickly, but this one seemed elusive, no solid leads. Hopefully, the capsule would give them some clues. She walked straight to the boardroom.

Thornberry stood looking outward, silhouetted by the bright sunlight that streamed in through the windows. She turned at the creak of the door.

"Hi, boss. How's it going?"

"I'm good." Flint's gaze drew away from the corporal and landed on the capsule. The light played on its polished surface, sending spirals of rainbows across the ceiling and walls. She wondered what secrets it held. Today they would find out.

"The rest of the team should be here any minute now," Thornberry said. She sat in her chair, opened the lid of her laptop and booted it up.

"Okay." Flint wandered over to the window and looked at the castle in the distance. "The light up is tonight."

"Jarrett and I are going."

"Me, too. My whole family actually," Flint said. "We're having dinner first. My mom got us window seats."

"Nice. Maybe, we'll see you there."

Flint sat down, glad that the corporal hadn't asked if Neil was joining them. Just another reminder of the bad situation she felt squeezing her. She pressed on her forehead to keep the headache at bay.

Just then the front door banged open. Hurried footsteps approached, one set light and springy followed by a slightly heavier tread.

Greenwood popped her head in the doorway.

"All right. Today is the day." The constable flopped into a chair and placed a notebook on the table. "Ready."

"Hey." Hay plodded into the room, pulled a chair aside and sat down.

"Who wants the honours?" Flint asked, looking around at her team.

"I'll do it," Hay said.

"Okay. By the way, did Ryan say anything when he dropped this off?" Flint asked.

"He said everything on the desk was put back in," Hay said. "He also showed me how to open it."

"Okay. Let's see what we got," Flint said.

Hay stood up and strolled down to the other side of the table. He put on the white gloves and picked up the special wrench left by the forensic scientist. They watched as he unscrewed each bolt and placed it beside the capsule. It took a while but finally the last of the sixteen bolts were removed.

"Hurry up," Greenwood said.

"It's not my fault. Ryan tightened the nuts way too much," Hay said. "We're almost there." He placed his large hand on the container and pulled off the cap. There was a sucking sound as the seal released, like the snap of a new jar of pickles being opened. He peered into the cylinder. "What do you want me to do?"

"I think it would be okay to empty the contents onto the table," Flint said. "But first, have we got a tablecloth or something soft we can put down?"

Thornberry jumped up and rummaged through the cupboards. She pulled out a checkered cloth, its edges frayed, and held it up.

"Perfect," Flint said.

After everything was set up, Hay tilted the capsule carefully and let the items spill out.

"You should do the honours, boss," Hay said and sat down at his regular spot.

"Sure." Flint stood up and walked to the head of the table. She glanced over the items. "It would be helpful if we had a contents list of the objects that are supposed to be in here."

"Ryan didn't say anything about a list," Hay said.

"Maybe Charles has it," Greenwood said. "You know, for safekeeping."

"That makes sense." Flint pulled out her cell phone and dialled the old man. After ten rings she gave up. "No answer. That's kind of weird. He's always home."

"Maybe there's a copy in the manager's office," Thornberry said.

"Can't hurt to try," Flint said.

Paulie answered on the third ring. As she listened, the expression on her face changed to one of chagrin. She hung up and swiped her hand across her forehead.

"What's wrong?" Hay asked.

"Jesus. Charles had a heart attack. He's in the hospital."

They sat in silence for a moment before Greenwood spoke up.

"What about the list?"

"He doesn't know anything about that," Flint said. "So let's move on for now. We can come back to that. Could someone take notes as we go through the stuff?"

"I will," Greenwood said.

The first item the sergeant picked up was a yellowed newspaper. A cloudy plastic wrap was wound around it in several layers. Flint had to squint to read the date. The picture on the top half of the fold was a black and white print.

"Okay. We have the *Province* paper from Vancouver. The year is 1980. I can't read the rest, but it looks like March 27. We can always look this up if it's important. Although, I don't know how this would connect with a murder now."

"So what is it exactly?" Greenwood asked.

"Right. It's the day Mount St. Helens erupted. It's a volcano in Washington state. The headline says it sent ash as far away as Vancouver."

"Wow. Cool," Greenwood said. "I guess only Hay is old enough to remember that." She nudged his elbow.

"I'm not that old," Hay said and pushed back.

"Can anyone think of how this would have any bearing on our investigation?" Flint glanced over the team who were shaking their heads. "We'll put that aside and move on."

The next item was a stack of photos tied together with a red ribbon.

"This looks more promising." Flint untied the bow and laid the pictures side by side so everyone could take a good look.

There were several photos of buildings taken on the main street in downtown Castlecrest. The Seabreeze Cafe looked exactly the same as it did today, even the sign hadn't been changed, only more weathered. The bank building had advertisements with interest rates posted in the window.

"Shit. Is that the mortgage rate? Sixteen percent? You're kidding, right?" Greenwood said.

"Inflation," Hay said. "That must be the opening of the movie theatre." He pointed to a photo where a line of people stretched down the sidewalk and around the corner from a building with a large marquee at the front.

"Do you know anybody?" Greenwood asked.

"Okay, you guys. Let's move on," Flint said. "The rest of these photos are just buildings except for this one at City Hall. There's a group of people, but the image is too small to really know who they are. Although, I think that's Charles at the end."

Flint set the photos to one side and chose the next item. It was a wind-up watch set at midnight. She flipped it over to see if there was an engraving. But no. It was just a watch. She supposed if fifty years had gone by before the capsule had been opened, it would seem quite illuminating, a glimpse into the past before everything was digital. She glanced over to Greenwood, but she didn't seem to have any interest in the watch.

There were some metals and coins. They examined some metals from both World War I and II and a 1980s Canadian Arctic Territories Centennial Specimen Silver Dollar Coin in a Royal Canadian Mint black clamshell case. Flint wondered if Charles or his father had something to do with the Arctic.

They looked at the next items quickly. A magazine showed the fashion trends of the time. The spandex and leg warmers made Flint gag. There were a few voter buttons from the federal election that year and a clipping from a paper declaring the winner. There were several grocery receipts. At this one, Thornberry couldn't believe how cheap food was.

"What the hell is this?" Greenwood groaned at the cassette tapes, although she did recognize one of the songs by Pink Floyd.

"Well, that's that," Flint said. She leaned on the table. "Does anybody have anything to say?"

"I don't see anything here pertinent to our investigation," Hay said.

"It sure appears that way," Flint said. "But I have a feeling something is missing. Somebody has stolen something…"

"Only Harris had access to the capsule," Thornberry said.

"Well, we don't know that for sure," Flint said. "And as I have said before, we don't know who was in the study that day. If a contents list even exists, Charles would be the person who had it."

"I agree," Greenwood said.

"Well, all we can do at this point is wait until Charles recovers," Flint said. "Let me call Dr. Lane and see what the situation is."

It was a quick call to the doctor. After hanging up, Flint smiled.

"He didn't have a heart attack. It was a panic attack," the sergeant said. And she knew how that felt, having experienced a panic attack herself. Several times. "Charles will be in the hospital for another night for observation. Dr. Lane thought it was a good idea that the old man had some company."

"What a tough old bugger," Greenwood said.

"I'm off," Flint grabbed her jacket and stood up.

"What should we do?" Thornberry asked.

"Catalogue all the items. Photos, descriptions. Write up a report, as well."

"Okay."

"And get some lunch."

* * *

Flint stopped at the deli for a sausage roll and then headed to the hospital. She parked in the visitor area and walked through the automatic sliding doors to the reception desk. The clerk directed her to a private room on the second floor. She turned left after exiting the elevator and immediately noticed the beautiful paintings on the walls reflecting the character of the town, the surrounding forest, the ocean and all the wildlife that lived in tandem with the residents. She lingered for a while, admiring a watercolour that reminded her of the beach by her parents' house, and then continued along the corridor.

Flint came to stop in front of a partially open door and knocked before entering. Charles sat upright on the bed gazing at the ceiling. He turned when she cleared her throat.

"How are you feeling?"

"I'm okay. Just a silly old man," he said. "Come in."

Flint looked around the room for somewhere to sit. Two leather chairs were pushed against the far wall. She pulled one up closer to the bed beside a small table loaded with flowers. Without preamble, she cut through the small talk and went directly to the heart of the matter.

"We opened the capsule this morning. I think that something might be missing."

"I'm not surprised," Charles said. "Is that why my boy was killed?"

"There's no evidence that the capsule has any bearing on what happened," Flint said. "But we're checking out everything."

"You know it was my wife's idea."

"What, the capsule?"

"Yes. She organized the whole thing and arranged all the contents. There was a committee, but she took charge." He glanced at the detective. "I think my wife put something in it. I don't know what. Don't ask, don't tell. That was my motto. Now I wish I knew."

Flint remained silent. The old man turned to her once again.

"Did you find anything that seemed odd?"

"No. What do you mean?"

"Nothing. I just had the impression she was keeping something from me. Forget it. I'm an old man with fanciful ideas." Charles leaned back into his pillow. "I miss her."

"I wondered if you had a list of the items that were put inside the capsule?" Flint asked.

"As it happens, I do." Charles paused. "I put it in my jacket pocket before I went to see Harris." He pointed to the closet in the corner. "Look in there."

Flint got up and opened the locker. She rummaged through the pockets until she found an envelope. "Is this it?" She held it up.

"Yeah, that's it," Charles said.

"Thank you. If we find anything, you'll be the first to know," Flint said. "Take care now."

After leaving the old man, Flint sat on a bench in front of the elevator and opened the envelope. She unfolded a hand-written note in flowery script inside and glanced down the list. And there it was. The very last item, the missing item.

A key.

Was this the object Mrs. Crest put in the capsule? What did it mean? And where was it now?

Chapter 15

Flint rushed back to the station. As she walked down the hallway, she could hear the low murmur of talk and laughter through the gap in the doorway. She stepped closer and smelt the sweet fragrance of coffee.

"Is this the mice will play thing going on here?" Flint asked as she pushed her way into the room.

"We have pastry, too," Thornberry said.

"So what happened?" Hay asked.

"You tell me," Flint said as she pulled the envelope from her pocket and handed it over to the constable. She headed over to the counter and grabbed a coffee and Danish before sitting down.

Hay scanned the note. "Oh, my God. A key is missing."

"Let me see." Thornberry grabbed at the paper and took a look. "A key. To what?"

"We had a good talk about the capsule," Flint said. She told them everything he had said about his wife.

"Do you think Mrs. Crest wrote the list?" Greenwood asked.

"I think so. Apparently, she arranged the whole thing," Flint said. "I don't know for a fact, but I have a feeling it was Mrs. Crest who decided to put the key in there."

"Where is it? Did someone steal it?" Hay asked.

"And what does it unlock?" Greenwood asked.

"That's a lot of questions," Flint said.

"But first we have to find it. Without the key, we'll never know the answers to any of our questions," Thornberry said.

"She's right. There's no way to know if any of this has anything to do with our investigation." Flint paused. "Unless we find what has been locked away."

"So how do we do that?" Greenwood asked. "It seems to me an impossible task."

"Let's take a step back and make some assumptions. We need a starting point," Flint said. "One. We know Harris was in the study all morning with the capsule. Two. We know several people entered the study that morning."

"Does that mean the killer has the key?" Greenwood asked.

"That's one possibility," Flint said.

"I don't see how it could be anybody else except the killer," Thornberry said.

"What's another option?" Greenwood asked.

"Somebody saw the key and thought it might open something of value."

"What? Are you saying someone stole it right from under Harris's nose?" Greenwood asked.

"Not exactly," Flint said. "Maybe the person took it after Harris was dead."

"Oh, shit. That's sick," Thornberry said.

"So let's make a list of people we know who were there."

"Mia was there," Hay said. "We only have her word that she didn't enter the room."

"Okay. That's good. Keep it going," Flint said.

"Paulie. We know he was in the room. He admitted it," Thornberry said.

"What about Bryson?" Greenwood said, happy to have some input.

"That's a possibility. Has anyone gotten a hold of him yet?" Flint asked.

"No, boss," Hay said.

"Okay. I hate to say this but there is one other person we know who was in the study that morning," Flint said.

"Who?" Thornberry asked.

"Charles."

"What? That's nuts," Thornberry said.

"Not so crazy. He admitted his wife might have been hiding something from him. Possibly something that would be embarrassing if it got out. I'm thinking he saw the key and freaked out," Flint said.

"That would mean the key has nothing to do with the murder then," Hay said.

"I'm puzzled about something. Why would Charles give us the list? That would just tell us about the missing key. Are you following me on this?" Thornberry asked.

"That makes sense. We'll rule Charles out for the time being. We can always get back to him if more evidence warrants it. He wasn't trying to hide anything from us. He gave us the list," Flint said. "Anybody else?"

"What about the gardener?" Greenwood asked. "She admitted she was working in the garden there. Maybe Harris invited her in to see the capsule. You know, bragging about it. She slips the key into her hand and he doesn't notice."

"I've felt as if she was holding back on something. Maybe we should bring her into the station. That'll get her talking," Flint said.

"Dr. Lane was in the study, as well," Hay said.

"Okay. What's the count at now?"

"Five people," Greenwood said.

"Okay. I have to say of the five, Bryson interests me the most. He seems to be ghosting us. Do we agree?"

The team all nodded in agreement.

"It's getting late. Let's call it a day and start fresh in the morning."

After everyone left the room, the sergeant made a phone call to Bryson's house. He wasn't home yet, but this time his wife relented and let her know he was expected back that evening.

Flint locked up the station and headed home. She planned on making a surprise visit to Bryson's house first thing in the morning. Really early. He had flown under the radar so far, but his time was up.

Chapter 16

As Flint arrived home, dusk was fast approaching, the last of the sun rays dancing on the horizon. With a blink, the sun disappeared in a final blaze of orange. As she walked down the sidewalk to the back door, she realized that every light in the house was on and shook her head knowing full well what was going on inside. But it was a good thing. They rarely went out all together for an evening event, so everyone would be in super excited mode. She smiled to herself, thankful for the pleasant change of pace. Even the cast on her daughter's arm would be forgotten for the moment.

The moment Flint opened the door, she could hear the ruckus coming from upstairs. Her dad sat quietly at the kitchen table with a cup of tea in front of him.

"They can't decide what to wear," Victor said.

"I better go see what's going on."

"You haven't got much time," her dad said, glancing at his watch. "Our reservations are for six. Light up at seven thirty."

"I heard there's going to be fireworks, as well," Flint said.

"You'll never get Paige to sleep tonight."

"She'll be vibrating. That's for sure," Flint said.

She crept up the stairs, peeping into her daughter's room for all of one minute before she was discovered.

"Mommy's here," Paige shrieked. She ran to the doorway and flung her arms around her mom's legs. And just as suddenly, she pulled away and pirouetted to show off her dress.

"You look beautiful," Flint said as she directed her gaze toward the bed loaded with, at a guess, almost every outfit Paige owned. She glanced sideways at her mom and asked in a hushed tone, "Final choice?"

"Still to be determined," Oleane whispered back.

"I better go get ready," Flint said. "I'll be quick."

She hurried out of the room before she could be further detained. After her shower, she chose black cargo pants and a thick grey wool turtleneck sweater. She tied her hair into a low ponytail and dabbed on some cherry lip gloss before heading downstairs.

The family was in the front foyer, bundling up for the chilled night. Scarves, gloves and hats were everywhere.

Paige was wearing her best black patent shoes, black tights and a knee-length red coat that was buttoned up to her neck. Her multi-coloured toque, knitted by her grandmother, was pulled down over her ears and touched the back of her collar. Wispy blonde strands of hair peeked out at the front. She stood with her hands on her hips, waiting impatiently for the adults.

Flint slipped on a black jacket and the same multi-coloured toque as Paige.

"I think we're ready," Oleane said and opened the door.

A blast of Arctic air blowing off the ocean met them full force. They quickly hopped into the Range Rover with Paige leading the pack. Victor had started up the vehicle ten minutes before, so it was toasty warm inside. He waited for everyone to buckle up before he backed out of the driveway.

After driving through town, Victor headed up the long road to the castle. The building appeared in the distance as he rounded the last curve. A few minutes later, he pulled into a brightly lit parking lot and came to a halt under a tall lamp.

Without hesitation, and in spite of the cold, they tumbled out of the car and scurried down the path to the front entrance. Two elves met them at the door and directed them to the dining area. Although the holidays were still weeks away, a decorated tree was on display in the foyer. It was nearly five metres tall and still did not reach the ceiling. They climbed the stairs to the second floor, the banister wrapped in fir boughs and ribbon. The scent of the forest mixed with the smell of food wafting from the restaurant.

"How lovely," Flint said. She held onto her daughter's hand and squeezed it gently.

After liberating themselves from their bulky outerwear, they were seated by the floor-to-ceiling windows with a big sky vista. The moon rode low in the south-west, and there were thousands, if not millions, of stars glimmering high above them. It was nights like this that Flint scanned the northern reaches for the aurora borealis, a rare occasion so far south, but nevertheless, in a perfect setting they would show up unannounced. She squinted her eyes to see better and thought there was just a hint of dancing green light. Below her feet, the lawn spread out in front of her. From this vantage point, Flint could see the cottages over the ridge and the garden sheds still partially hidden behind the trees.

"We're going to have a great view of the fireworks from here," Flint said.

But nobody was listening to her. Her dad stared out the window, attracted to something she couldn't see. Her mom was too busy trying to get Paige to sit still. So Flint sat back to enjoy her moment of peace and a glass of wine from the complementary bottle set on the table. Not the best, but it was working its magic.

Flint glanced around the room. It was a grand space to say the least. The tallest of ceilings, circular wood tables with floral centrepieces, sandalwood candles, sparkling silverware and the best China. It was exquisite.

Flint stretched her neck and could just make out Jarrett and Thornberry seated at the far end, sitting across from one another, not seeing much of anything except each other. He wore a short-sleeve shirt to show off his ripped biceps. She had on a classic black dress with pearls around her neck. They made a nice couple, although Flint never saw that coming.

Flint twisted in her seat and looked over her shoulder. Paulie was talking to a group of older women one table over. He gave a little wave of acknowledgement when she caught his eye. She nodded back and returned her attention to her family, taking another sip of her wine. Her dad winked at her.

Not long after everyone finally settled, a waitress approached their table. It was Mia.

"Oh. Hi, Sergeant Flint," Mia said.

"Hello," Flint said. "The place looks wonderful."

"Are you enjoying the wine?" she asked. "It's on the house tonight."

"I think we should order something special," Victor said and glanced over to his daughter.

Flint grinned at him.

"Of course. Have you got something in mind?" Mia asked.

"Something full-bodied. Maybe a Merlot from the Okanagan," Victor said.

"We have an extensive selection," Mia said and handed the wine list to him.

Victor perused the list for several moments then looked up at the waitress. "I heard rumours there is still wine stocked from when the castle was first built."

"Yeah, apparently they opened a few bottles from the original cellar. Unfortunately, the wine had turned to vinegar."

"That's never good."

"Dad. How about a nice red from the Oliver region," Flint interrupted. "Maybe a Nota Bene from Black Hills Estate."

"That will do," Victor said.

"And something for the youngster?" Mia asked.

"Maybe a small pop," Flint said.

"Okay. I'll be right back." Mia turned and hurried toward the kitchen.

"She seems like a nice girl," Oleane said.

"Yes," Flint said and changed the subject immediately. No need to talk about a witness, although her mother wouldn't be wise about that. "So what are we going to order for food?"

"Can I have fish and chips?" Paige asked.

"Okay. I think I'll have the salmon," Flint said without even looking at the menu. "What about you, Mom?"

"Same here. The salmon."

"I suppose, you'll be ordering a steak." Flint glanced at her dad.

"We are so predictable," Victor said.

In short time, the wine was uncorked, and the meal was served. The food lived up to their expectations. The conversation was light and airy. Flint felt content to sit idly with her family. Towards the end of the feast, she saw Thornberry and Jarrett leave the dining area. She figured they were headed out for a little intimate time before all the activities started.

"The fireworks will be starting soon," Mia said when she came back to check on whether they needed anything else. "Perhaps you might be interested in some dessert? The double-layered chocolate cake is to die for."

"I think we're good," Flint said, grimacing at the waitress's choice of words. She glanced around the table but nobody had noticed.

"What about the light up?" Oleane asked as she turned away from wiping her granddaughter's chin.

"That will happen after the fireworks. It gives everyone a chance to finish up and get outside to enjoy it fully."

"Of course."

"I don't think we need anything else. Just the damages," Victor said, grinning. "Thank you."

Mia tapped on her tablet. She placed the bill on the table and walked away.

Flint looked up as the first flash of the fireworks lit the sky, followed by a loud bang. And then a succession of bursts went off, one after the other.

Paige squealed with delight.

Flint watched as the colourful sparks rained down upon the lawn. As her gaze lowered, she spotted Jarrett walking over the ridge toward the cottages. Thornberry had stopped several metres away to look up at the fireworks.

A flicker of light caught Flint's eye. Was she seeing things? No. There was definitely something not quite right.

She stood up.

"What's wrong?" Victor asked.

"I think there's a fire."

"Where?" Victor asked, then turned in the direction of his daughter's stare.

The fire sprung to life in a wash of orange and yellow sparks.

"Look. There's someone running," Flint said.

An explosion rattled the windows.

"What the hell," Victor swore.

"Oh, my God. Jarrett."

Within moments, Harris's cottage was engulfed in flames and raging out of control.

Flint sprinted out of the castle like the devil was chasing her.

Chapter 17

The explosion had thrown Jarrett metres away from where he had been standing. He was a crumpled heap amidst the chaos. Burning bits of debris from the cottage littered the lawn. Even the surrounding trees had not escaped the inferno, their low-hanging branches singed at the tips from the intense flames.

Flint ran down the stairs and out the door. As she neared the blaze, she could feel the heat on her bare arms. A plume of black smoke belched from the burning building, filling her nostrils with an acrid smell.

Thornberry knelt beside the constable, tears welling in her eyes. "He's not responsive, but at least he's breathing."

"That's a good sign," Flint said, kneeling across from the corporal. She ran her hands along Jarrett's body to check for wounds talking all the while in a low voice, not sure if he could hear her. But if he did, it would have a soothing effect on him. When her fingers reached his chest, he jerked.

Flint stopped and sat back on her heels.

"What is it?" Thornberry asked frantically. "Is he okay?"

"I think there are a few broken ribs. We better not move him." The sergeant wasn't sure if there were more injuries.

Thornberry went quiet.

Flint glanced around and saw her dad standing by the cottage, shooing the crowd away. Sirens wailed in the distance, coming ever closer. The heat on their backs grew more intense as the fire raged behind them, the stiff wind whipping up the flames.

With one last whoop, loud and close, an eerie void filled the gap. Flint could hear the sound of the crackling fire and the hushed whispers in the air. Then the stomping coming toward them like a thousand horses thundering over the ridge.

"They're here. Hang on. Everything will be okay." Flint looked down at the constable and saw his eyelids flicker.

In a matter of moments, the paramedics loaded the semi-conscious Jarrett onto a stretcher, wrapping him in blankets, and secured him for the bumpy hike up the hill to the waiting ambulance. They hoisted him into the back of the vehicle and placed an oxygen mask over his chalk white face. Thornberry scrambled in and sat beside him on a tiny jump seat. She looked down on his fragile body, blinking repeatedly to stop the tears.

As the ambulance sped away Flint was left standing alone in the darkness.

Then the firemen arrived, in groups of twos and threes, weighted down by all their gear, the metal clanging as they jogged. Their faces reflected their strength, a determination and a single-minded pursuit. There was a harmony to the noise and commotion as hoses were stretched out across the lawn and down the slope. The first blast of water hissed as it hit the flames, sending a dense mass of smoke into the trees.

Flint pulled her hand over her mouth and closed her eyes momentarily. Over the hill, she saw three figures approach with quickening steps. She couldn't remember the last time she was so glad to see these men, the uniformed officers from her station. They huddled in close to the sergeant, touching shoulders, joined as a whole.

"We only have one job to do," Flint said. "We need to find the villain who harmed one of our own."

And as they stood up straight and nodded, Flint wondered what the hell was in the cottage that someone wanted to hide so badly? What had they missed?

Chapter 18

In the end, the crew took two hours to put out the blaze, leaving behind just a shell of a house and a heap of smouldering ash. The hunt for the arsonist came up empty. They had searched along the waterfront to the next property and beyond, but whoever Flint had seen running was obviously long gone. No clues at all. No visible car tracks, no imprints in the dirt. Disappointed but realistic, she thanked the officers and sent them home. Although she was exhausted both mentally and physically, she hung around. She talked to the firemen and kicked around the outskirts of the crime scene, absorbed in her thoughts. There was nothing more she could do. The ashes were too hot to explore, and anyway that would be a job for the fire chief who was out of town until the morning.

Flint found out a few things from the firemen who remained, so it wasn't a total waste of time. They couldn't officially make a determination, but as one of them explained it was a chain reaction. A pile of discarded oily rags beside the propane tank had been set on fire and ignited the whole kit and kaboodle. It had literally become a bomb.

Flint stared at the hot spot the fireman had pointed out to her but couldn't really make anything out. It looked like one big, soggy mass of burnt stuff. Finally, feeling despondent, she left the scene and headed up the hill.

Flint called a cab. She waited under the portico and checked her messages again. Thornberry had called earlier to say Jarrett was in surgery. She had also texted several times with no news, just an update that the doctors were still working on him. Each text sounded more desperate than the last. All Flint could do was lamely text back with words of encouragement that she didn't really feel.

Flint glanced at her watch and decided not to call Thornberry until the morning. The corporal was probably sleeping in a chair in the waiting room. The cab arrived and dropped her off at home. Only the back porch light was on, even her dad had given up hope on her coming in at a half decent hour. She gave the dog a scratch behind his ear and peeked into the living room out of habit. She was surprised to see her dad slumped in his favourite chair in the dark. He stirred when she walked into the room.

"Come tell me what happened," Victor said. He sat up, switched on a lamp and stretched his back.

"Honestly, Dad. You didn't have to wait up for me. It's four in the morning."

"Well in that case, we should put some coffee on," Victor said. "Don't you think?"

"I do." Flint agreed.

They sat across from each other at the table. Flint set a plate of cookies out to dunk into her drink.

"How's Jarrett doing?"

"So far so good." Flint shrugged. "I haven't heard from Thornberry in a while."

"He'll pull through."

"It was damn lucky he wasn't killed," Flint said and sighed. "We weren't able to catch up with the culprit who started the fire."

"I guess there aren't any security cameras in that area."

"There aren't any cameras at the hotel," Flint said. "So I would be surprised if there were any at the cottages."

"Really? The parking lot has them."

"What?"

"Well, there was quite the line-up of vehicles to get out of the place after the explosion. It was a crawl through the parking lot. I noticed cameras up on the lamp standards," Victor said.

"That's crazy. The manager told us there weren't any." Flint pressed her lips together. "What an asshole. What's his game, I wonder?"

"Maybe they're not functional."

"I'll find out tomorrow," Flint said, settling back into her chair.

"You mean today?"

"Yeah." Flint dipped the last bit of her cookie into the coffee and gulped it down.

"Are Paige and Mom okay?"

"Paige thought it was cool."

"Oh, to be so innocent," Flint said. "And Mom?"

"She's all right. A bit of a shock."

Flint nodded.

"You should try to get a few hours' sleep," Victor said. "Me, too." He stood up and placed his empty mug on the counter.

They headed up the stairs.

"Thanks, Dad."

"Goodnight." Victor walked to his bedroom, closing the door softly behind him.

Flint stole a glance into her daughter's room. Paige was sprawled across the bed, legs entwined in the blankets. Normal stuff. She smiled and went to her room. She curled up on a cushion in the bay window and stared out to sea, trying to stop her mind from working overtime. The moon had risen in the sky but was partially hidden by steel grey clouds that had gathered overnight and threatened rain. She thought about everything that had happened today, but nothing made any sense. Harris's cottage had been worked over by the forensics team more than once. There was nothing to be found, unless they were looking at things the wrong way.

The next thought that struck Flint shook her to the core. What if the person had meant to burn down Charles's cottage? With the old man in it? Had it just been bad luck on the arsonist's part that they had picked the wrong cottage? And on top of that, wasn't it strange that a person who would want to harm the old man not know that he was in the hospital and not at home? Wouldn't the person be privy to all these facts? Their mistakes were a lucky break for Charles.

Flint rubbed at her temple, feeling the throbbing beneath her fingers. She fell asleep but woke up after only a few hours with her thoughts picking up where she had left off. As hard as she tried, she found it impossible to get back to sleep. So she got up, took a long, hot shower, grabbed a coffee and headed to the station instead.

* * *

Paulie had been as surprised as anyone by the explosion. He radioed to the fireworks crew on the ground to stop. People were fleeing the restaurant, so he didn't have to make any announcements about postponing the light up. It took several hours to clean up and send the employees home. He was too frazzled to set off, so he sat in his office and mulled over everything that had happened. The key sat on his desk. He touched the cold metal with his finger, trying to remember something he had heard that evening. He had the notion it was important, but the thought lingered just outside his comprehension. He unlocked the bottom drawer and placed the key at the back, covering it with brochures. After locking everything up, he left for home.

Chapter 19

Flint heard thunder in the distance as the first raindrops began to fall, noisily clattering as they hit the glass pane. She sat at her desk and watched as the clouds moved in closer. Within a few minutes the rain pelted down in sheets, so she could barely see out the window. She turned her attention back to the murder book opened to the first page. She thought about Harris, the heir to the Crest fortune. No wife. No kids. Was there a girlfriend? Nobody had mentioned that. There were so many reasons that a person killed. Money, greed, secrets best kept hidden. Where was jealousy on the list? She jotted a note on a pink Post-it note to check that out.

A loud, deep resounding noise made Flint look up. It wasn't more thunder, but doors being slammed and people banging around. The strides approaching from the south foyer seemed over-loud in the quiet station. She waited.

"Superintendent." Flint jumped out of her chair when a man stopped at the doorway.

Allen Gill was dressed in full uniform, as usual. There seemed to be more streaks of grey in his black hair than the last time she had seen him. His large figure was dwarfed by the man who accompanied him.

"Sit. Sit," Gill said. "I'm sorry you have to meet the new fire chief under the circumstances." He sat on a chair in front of her desk.

The fire chief was younger than Flint had imagined. He had long, blonde hair that curled at his ears. His mischievous eyes sparkled in spite of the firm, unwavering set of his jaw, as if he knew something you didn't. He reached out his arm and shook hands with her. It was a strong grip, conveying grit and determination, someone who wouldn't back down in adverse situations.

"Tim Miles."

"Nice to meet you finally," Flint said and smiled.

"So I got in quite early this morning and went straight to the crime scene," Tim started without preamble. "I can tell you the gist of my findings. There wasn't any forensic evidence which indicated that an accelerant had been used. A cigarette butt was the likely start of the fire. And before you ask, the fire was too hot and destroyed all traces of prints or DNA. Sorry about that. And the rest of it, the explosion, well that was just unfortunate. Although it takes quite a bit to blow up a propane tank, there were two circumstances at work here. The first was having a fire right next to the relief valve on the tank. The second is an educated guess, but I think we can assume the valve was probably worn-out and had a slight leak. That happens in these old tanks. So in my mind, it was a careless act of discarding a still lit butt on top of a pile of oily rags on a windy night. I will email the report to you when I get back to my office."

"Could the person have deliberately tossed the lit cigarette on the rags to get the fire going?" Flint asked.

"Sure. But as I explain in my report, it was a dark night and no moonlight to speak of. So unless the person knew the rags were there and the valve just above them, as well..." Tim shrugged. "Like I said. Your call. I just give you the facts. You do the detecting. I will leave that for you to decide once you've read the full report." His blue eyes glinted.

"Thanks for coming by," Flint said.

"No problem," Tim said and stood up. "I have to be on my way now. Talk to you again. Call me if you have any further questions."

After the fire chief left, Gill spoke up. "Have you got a suspect?"

"We're honing in on someone," Flint said. Then to clarify her remarks, she added, "For the murder. I'm not sure if the fire is part of the investigation at this point, although we will definitely look into it." She stopped talking and glanced at the superintendent, hoping her countering statements weren't too noticeable.

Gill nodded his head. "You let me know if there is anything I can do."

Flint listened to his footsteps fade away before she sat back in her chair and Greenwood popped her head in the doorway.

"Holy shit. That was crazy," Greenwood said. "Is Jarrett okay? Are you okay?"

"Yeah, yeah, don't worry about me. I spoke to Thornberry earlier. The surgery went well, but Jarrett won't be coming back to work for a while."

"Oh." Greenwood pressed her lips together, suppressing a smile.

"I know you want Jarrett to get better," Flint said. "I may keep you on even when he gets back on the job."

"Am I that obvious?" Greenwood shrugged.

"Yeah, you are," Flint said. "Look, we have lots to do. First up, you and me are going to have a serious chat with Bryson."

"Hey, what about me?" Hay strolled into the room and sat down. "What? Am I chopped liver now?"

"I have a special job for you," Flint said. "My dad noticed cameras in the parking lot at the castle last night."

"Whoa! Paulie lied to us," Greenwood said.

"Not necessarily. We only asked if there were cameras around the castle." Flint paused. "Maybe he was being a little cagey."

"Right," Hay said. "Or he's trying to hide something."

"Well, go shake him down then," Flint said, laughing. "Get the videos and see what you can find."

"Okay."

"Look for a blue Bronco, as well," Flint said.

"What's up?" Hay asked.

"That's what Bryson drives." Flint smiled. "Kim said he was there, so let's find out if he lied to us or she was confused."

"Good one, boss," Hay said.

Greenwood snickered.

Flint knew Thornberry would have loved this assignment, but she was taking some time to spend with Jarrett while he was recuperating. The corporal had grown up with technology and knew it well. Some would say she knew computers inside and out. However, what was at hand was quite simple. All Hay had to do was sit at a desk and watch a video. He didn't have to make the picture clearer or better. It all came down to placing the Bronco in the parking lot at the right time.

The detectives stood up in unison.

"I'm glad to see we're anxious to get this show on the road," Flint said. "We finally have some direction."

They walked side by side down the hallway.

"I'll bet Jarrett isn't coming back," Hay said.

Flint glanced at Greenwood. She had her head hung down, ignoring the constable's remark. When they got outside, they parted company. The clouds had scuttled away, leaving a freshness in the air and a blue sky.

Hay hopped into his vehicle and headed up to the castle to confront Paulie about the video.

Flint drove north to the edge of town where all the houses were on large lots and hidden from view by tall hedges. The boulevard trees spread their arms over the wide streets, meeting in the centre to form a tunnel. In the summer, the foliage cast shadows of light and dark. Now the bare branches dappled with lichen formed a beautiful mosaic against the sky. She pulled into a driveway on the right, an intricate wrought iron gate fashioned off the pattern of the trees blocking the way. She rolled down her window and reached over to the intercom.

Nobody answered but a buzzer sounded, and the gates swung open. Flint drove down the tree-lined driveway to a large two-storey house. The focal point at the front was a fountain with bronze fish spouting water from their mouths. The sound of the trickling water was somewhat soothing to her jangled nerves. Flint stopped to look down into the pool and saw goldfish darting among the water lilies.

The round top double doors were made from a hardwood that Flint had never seen before. After she rang the bell, through the clear bevelled glass she could see someone approach the entrance. A plump woman dressed in a blue wool skirt and white cashmere sweater with a multi-coloured scarf around her neck greeted them.

"Come in. Bryson is in the lounge." She turned quickly and walked away.

The detectives followed her down the wide hallway. Small black-and-white photos and gilt-edged mirrors lined the grey walls. Ahead of them, the ocean came into view. In the sheltered bay, a small but expensive-looking boat moored to a short dock bounced with the waves.

"He's in here." The woman stopped at the second door and left them standing as she scurried away.

"Was that the missus?" Greenwood said. "What a snob."

"We'll find out," Flint said.

She tapped lightly on the door frame and stepped inside when someone shouted out. Bryson sat in front of a lit fireplace with a book in his hand. He put a marker between the pages and placed it on the table beside him.

"Bryson. Thank you for seeing us." Flint glanced outside and could just see the boat in her line of vision, the waves slapping against its hull.

"Sure. Although, I don't know what else I can tell you," he said. "Have a seat."

Flint sat opposite him in a wing chair. The leather was the softest she had ever felt. The space was decorated with eighteenth-century, maybe earlier, pottery vases. Several held fresh flowers that filled the air with a sweet scent. The hand-woven rugs and old faded tapestries that hung on the walls made the room palatial. What really set it off from humdrum rich was the highly polished grand piano in the corner. She wondered how this man managed to have the best of everything.

The constable took a seat with a view toward the dock and placed her notepad on her lap.

"We have a witness that places you at the castle right around the time of the murder," Flint said, her eyes fixed on the suspect.

"What? No way. Who?" Bryson stumbled over his words.

"A waitress said you bumped into her," Flint said and raised her eyebrows. "By the study door."

"She, whoever she is, has made a mistake," Bryson said. "I don't know any waitresses there."

"Regardless, she recognized you. So can you explain that?"

"I was at home like I already told you." Bryson sank back into the thick cushions.

"Can anyone vouch for you? Your wife?" Flint asked, unperturbed by his denial. Although truth be told, she wasn't totally convinced about Kim's fluctuating story about who she saw. Maybe she had made up the whole story. Fifteen minutes of fame.

"No, I was here on my own. My wife was out with friends."

"I just have a few more questions," Flint said. "Could you tell me where you were last night?"

"I was here, as usual," Bryson said. He tilted his head. "What's going on?"

"You didn't go to the light up at the castle?" Flint continued.

"Oh, the fire. No, I wasn't there, and I didn't have anything to do with it." Bryson paused. "Thank goodness Charles was in the hospital. All that smoke."

"Can your wife verify that you were home?"

"I'm afraid not. She was at her weekly bridge game." Bryson rubbed his hands together. "Look, Sergeant. I didn't have anything to do with the murder."

"Do you know what's in the capsule?" Flint changed subjects abruptly.

"Really? What does that have to do with anything?" Bryson asked. He stared at the sergeant. "No, I don't. I was there when it was dug up, but I have no idea what's in it."

"Okay."

"Am I missing something here?"

"No, just routine questions," Flint said.

Bryson kept his gaze on the sergeant.

Flint glanced sideways at the constable and frowned. With only a single unreliable witness, there wasn't anything more she could do. She had no more questions, no line of thought to keep this going.

"Was the lady who answered the door your wife?"

"Yes."

"We would like to have a word with her," Flint said.

"Martha was on her way out, so she'll have to get back to you," Bryson said.

"At her earliest convenience," Flint said. She stood up and placed her card on the table.

"I'll be sure to tell her." Bryson showed them to the door and watched as they headed down the driveway.

The metal gates banged behind them with a thud. Flint drove slowly down the street, mulling over the conversation with Bryson.

"What now?" Greenwood asked.

Before Flint could reply, her cell phone pinged. She pulled over on the boulevard and answered. "What's up?"

Flint listened for several minutes, her lips forming a thin line before breaking into a slow smirk. She let out a loud whoop after hanging up.

"What's going on?" Greenwood asked.

"That was Hay. He found the Bronco."

"Our Bronco? The blue one?"

"Yup and yup. And a good shot of Bryson getting into it."

"And?"

"Within the relevant time frame of when the murder took place."

"All right. Let's go get him."

"Oh, there's more," Flint said. She hit the steering wheel with the palm of her hand. "Hay has been around the block a couple of times, so he went right ahead and got us a search warrant. He's on his way here with it at this moment."

"Oh, boy. Some action," Greenwood said and hung onto the dashboard as the sergeant performed a three-point turn and drove back in the other direction.

They could hear a siren coming down the street. Soon blue lights came into view.

"There's Hay," Greenwood said as she turned in her seat to see the police car rushing in behind them.

The two vehicles parked at the entrance to Bryson's place. Flint hopped out and walked over to Hay's window. After a few minutes of consultation and a handing off of the warrant to the sergeant, the constable took off back to the station.

"Unfortunately, the judge would only sign off on a warrant for the development property. He said he would adjust it for the house and vehicles if we find anything," Flint said, getting back into the car.

"I guess we better find something then. Hadn't we?" Greenwood asked.

Flint nodded. She buzzed the intercom for the second time that day, but instead of the gates opening a tired voice asked, "Did you forget something?"

"We have a search warrant. Open the gate."

Chapter 20

Bryson stood in the doorway when they cruised up to the entrance.

"Wait here," Flint said to Greenwood. She leapt out of the vehicle and up the steps.

"What's this about?"

"There are cameras in the parking lot." Flint tapped the warrant papers on her thigh.

"Oh. I see." Bryson lowered his head.

"Why did you lie about being at the castle? Did you kill Harris?"

"No, I didn't kill him. It's not what you think," Bryson said, tugging on his collar.

"Tell me, what is it I think?"

"I only went there to ask him to put his grievances aside. For his dad's sake. And then I left."

Flint waited for him to say more. She kept her gaze steady.

"Look. He told me to get lost. That's it."

"So you didn't push him."

"No. We just talked."

"Okay. So if it was just a conversation, I'll ask again. Why didn't you tell us you were there when we asked?"

"I didn't want to get involved." Bryson sighed. "Look. I made a mistake. I should have told you."

"Yeah. It's a little late now," Flint said. She handed him the warrant. "It's to search your development property and the buildings on site."

"Sure. I have nothing to hide." Bryson pulled out some keys from his pocket and handed them over to her.

"We'll meet you there."

"I have things to do. I'll get my keys back later."

"Suit yourself," Flint said. She jingled the keys then stuck them in her pocket.

The detectives headed up the castle road, and then veered off to the left onto a road that would take them to Bryson's development next door. When Flint pulled into the gravelled area in front of the office, Hay was already there with two officers from their detachment. They stood in a semi-circle with their backs to the ocean. A steady breeze blowing across the frigid water made their faces red and their teeth chatter. They were in the middle of an animated discussion as she approached the group. Probably about sports, Flint thought. It was always hockey or football with these guys.

"Boss," Hay said. "Where do you want us to start?"

"Hello, everyone." Flint shivered from the cold. "I know it's not nice out here, but let's be thorough. We have one shot at it. If we don't find anything then this avenue of inquiry is lost." She pointed to the uniformed officers. "You two can check the entire grounds. Take extra care looking through the dune grass. It's easy to hide something there."

"What are we looking for?" one of the officers asked.

"A knife. We're looking for a knife. But if you find anything suspicious, bag it up."

"Okay, you got it," the officer replied. He headed to the berm that rose above the beach with the second uniform following in his tracks.

"There's a lot of discarded material around here," Flint said as she glanced around the yard. She put her hand up to forehead and scanned into the distance. "Do you know if there are any other structures on the premises?" She looked directly at Hay, knowing he would have scouted the property before she arrived.

"There's a couple of dilapidated sheds at the far end," he said. "They're barely standing."

"Okay. Why don't you start by combing through all this debris. And when you're finished with that take a better look at those other buildings."

"I'm on it."

"Don't go in if it's too dangerous," Flint said.

Hay nodded in agreement.

"Greenwood and I will sift through the documents in the office. Maybe we'll find something that could shed some light on motive."

"You bet." Hay pulled his jacket collar up to cover his ears. He began his search at the front, tossing aside old chairs and broken-down office equipment to get to the soggy garbage underneath.

"What a contrast between Bryson's house and here," Greenwood said. "Hay will probably find a few rat's nests."

"Ugh," Flint said, cringing at the garbage that was thrown anywhere and everywhere. And it smelt. She turned away, unlocked the door to the office and stepped into the small space. Inside wasn't much warmer than outside. She switched on the lights, and then looked around for some kind of furnace. Behind the desk, she found a wall-mounted electric heater. She set the thermostat to its highest, and immediately the fan kicked in.

"That's better," Flint said. She put her hands up to the warmth.

"It's going to take us a while to sort this mess out," Greenwood said as she looked around at all the boxes on the floor. "It doesn't look like anything is labelled."

"Have at it. I'll start with the file cabinet." Flint went over to the only new piece of furniture in the trailer, pulled open a drawer and plucked out the solitary folder. She sat behind the desk with the files and let the hot air blow on her back.

"Right. I'll get to it then," Greenwood said. She opened a carton and frowned as she traced her fingers down the stack of folders neatly piled inside. "There aren't any labels on these, either. Just some letters and numbers." She took a batch of the files and placed them on the corner of the desk, and then sat down on the only other chair in the room, a rickety folding chair.

Flint spent a half an hour rooting through the documents to no avail. She glanced at the constable. "Just receipts. No documents about sales. No bank statements."

"Maybe Bryson keeps the important stuff at home," Greenwood said.

"Well, they're not here."

"Away from prying eyes," the constable added.

"Are you having any luck?"

"Nope."

Flint replaced the thick folder into the cabinet and grabbed the next unopened carton.

As they worked through the boxes in search of anything that would point to a motive, they could hear Hay working his way around the building. The thumping at the back let them know how far along he had progressed with his own hunt. It didn't look good, Flint thought.

After four painstaking hours, they came to the end of the line, finding nothing of value to their investigation. There was a pile of letters addressed to prospective clients, some promising replies from persons interested in the upcoming development and even a few personal correspondences. Although those had no bearing on the case. Flint was surprised that there were absolutely no financial records of any kind.

"Bryson definitely keeps the important stuff at home," Flint murmured. "Not sure we can get a search warrant for the house."

"You'll think of something," Greenwood said as she stretched out her back. "I'm hungry. What about you?"

"Me, too. There's nothing here. Let's go."

Without warning, the door slammed hard against the wall and sent it rocking on its hinges. The detectives looked up at the intrusion.

"Sorry about that. The wind caught it," Hay said as he pulled the door shut. "I've gone through everything, but I've come up empty. Never in all my life have I seen so much junk. What the hell is he keeping all this stuff for?"

"What about the other guys? I'm guessing they didn't find anything either," Flint said.

"I just sent them home. It's getting too dark out to actually see anything."

"They can come back tomorrow. Although we only get one chance to look, the warrant didn't have a time frame."

"I felt sure I would find something," Hay said, disappointment in his voice.

"We were thinking of a bite to eat at the Seabreeze before wrapping it up for the day. Are you in?"

"Definitely, I could use a beer."

"Okay. Let's lock up," Flint said.

The motion detector light flashed on as they filed out of the office and stopped just outside the door.

"Hang on. I forgot to turn the heater off," Flint said and headed back in. As she reached for the thermostat, a loud, metallic clang rang out followed by more loud clashes. She charged outside to see what had caused the disturbance.

Both detectives stood away from the overturned burn barrel. Hay looked especially sheepish.

"What the hell happened?" Flint asked. "I thought the whole building was going to come down on my head."

"Damn thing," Hay said.

Flint glanced at Greenwood who just shrugged noncommittally.

"I lost my cool. Sorry," Hay said.

"You kicked the barrel over?" Flint glanced from Hay to the steel drum.

"I didn't think it was going to roll off its pad. I was frustrated. Don't worry, I'll fix it."

"Forget about it. Let's go," Flint said.

"Nah, I'll do it now. I'm such an ass." With a little effort Hay righted the barrel. A faint clink of metal on metal sounded. He looked at the other two. "Did you hear that?"

Flint and Greenwood crept in closer.

Hay pulled his flashlight off his duty belt and aimed the light into the barrel. He leaned over to see better. The powerful beam played along the bottom of the container. He couldn't quite make out what was sitting loosely on top of the hardened clump of ashes. Lacking any acrobatic skills, he leaned in further, his gut pressing against the side of the barrel. He grunted as he reached out, his hand groping for the object. With one last effort and a final grunt his fingers touched and then rested on the cool metal. He withdrew his arm and turned around to the others.

"What is it?" Greenwood asked.

The knife glinted in the dim light.

"Holy shit," Flint said.

"It's the murder weapon," Greenwood said.

"Oh yeah, we've got him now," Flint said.

Hay grinned.

"Bag it," Flint said.

She pulled her cell phone out of her pocket and hit the dedicated button for the forensic scientist. After a short conversation, she hung up.

"Ryan will meet you at the station. Greenwood and I will pick up Bryson," she said to Hay.

The siren resonated through the tall fir trees and faded beneath the crashing of the waves as Flint flew down the castle road, lights reflecting off the wet pavement. It was just a short jaunt through the side streets from there. When Flint reached Bryson's place, she switched off the siren, but let the lights flash in the gathering gloom. The gate was closed, so she pressed on the intercom. After a minute went by and nobody answered, she pressed again. This time she held her finger on the button longer.

"Nobody's answering," Flint said.

"What should we do?" Greenwood asked.

"We'll have to come back in the morning. We don't have an arrest warrant. We can only detain him for questioning until the DNA results come back."

"Okay," Greenwood said.

Flint called Hay and told him Bryson wasn't home, so all they could do was wait it out. She dropped Greenwood at the station to get her vehicle and left for home.

It had been a hell of a day. Flint was hungry, tired and pulsating with underlying tension. The break in the case had happened, and now it was hard to settle down.

Flint pulled into the driveway, turned off the ignition and listened to the soothing sounds of the waves in the distance. She hopped out of the car and scurried down the side path to the back door. The dog greeted her with a big yawn. Her parents sat at the kitchen table sipping tea and smiled at her when she entered the room.

"You look ragged," Oleane said.

"That's okay," Flint said. "It's been a productive day." She flung herself into a chair.

"Did you arrest someone?" Victor asked.

"Not yet, but we have a suspect," Flint said.

"Oh, that's nice, dear," Oleane said. "Sorry. I mean it worked out. Didn't it?"

"You mean you're glad it wasn't Neil." Flint patted her mom's hand. "Me, too."

"You need some food," her mom said. She got up, pulled a plate out of the oven and placed it in front of her daughter. "Eat."

They chatted for about an hour before Flint called it a night. She headed upstairs and tiptoed past her daughter's room, pausing for a brief moment to take a peek. All was well. It was a nightly routine that was comforting. Flint felt so lucky that her mom and dad were part of the nest. She took a quick hot shower, got into her pyjamas and slipped under the covers. If she had been counting backwards from one hundred, she would have made it to ninety-five.

Chapter 21

Flint stepped into the station just as the slight drizzle turned into a downpour. Fall and winter meant monsoons. She headed to the boardroom to see if anybody was in. Hay's laptop was open with a picture frozen on the screen. It was the video from the parking lot. She pressed the start button and watched Bryson bustle to his vehicle. It was a clear shot, unmistakable.

"Morning, boss," Hay said as he stepped into the room. "I printed up some stills for the interview."

"Bryson get picked up then?" Flint asked.

"Yes. About a half hour ago. He's in the holding cell."

"Great," Flint said. "What about the DNA results from the knife? What did Ryan say?"

"There's a bit of a backlog. He said to call him later this morning. He'll have a better idea."

"Rats. I'll phone up front and see when Bryson's lawyer is expected and go from there."

Flint spoke to the desk sergeant for several moments. She hung up and sank back into her chair. "You and me soon. He'll give us a call."

"Okay."

They heard the heavy tread of someone approaching from the hallway.

"Sounds like Thornberry," Hay said. He turned to see the corporal standing in the doorway. "You look like shit."

"I feel like shit," Thornberry said. She plopped into a chair and brushed back strands of wet hair from her face.

"How's Jarrett doing?" Flint asked.

"As good as can be expected," Thornberry said. "He really took a hit from the explosion. There were a number of broken ribs like you thought. His arm was broken in two places, as well."

"Ouch," Hay said.

The team sat in silence and listened as the wind whipped the rain mercilessly against the windowpanes. The entrance door slammed and moments later Greenwood entered the room.

"We did it." The constable stood in the doorway, shook off the rain from her jacket and placed a box of pastries on the table. She looked at the sour expression on Flint's face. "Did something happen?"

"No. I'm puzzled. What could be a possible motive for him?" Flint asked. "It's definitely not money. You saw his place. So what is it?"

"Maybe it's all on borrowed money," Greenwood said.

Flint shrugged. "Possibly."

"A personal vendetta?" Hay asked.

"Could be. We'll need to whittle it out of him," Flint said. She flipped open the murder book and scanned the last few pages, scribbling notes on a pad. The phone buzzed. "They're ready for us."

Greenwood jumped out of her chair. "Right on."

"Hay is coming with me this time," Flint said.

"Oh."

"You have a lot of paperwork to catch up on." Flint looked at the corporal. "I think you should go home and get some sleep."

"Thanks," Thornberry said. "I will. Soon."

"All right then."

Hay and the sergeant walked toward the south entrance where the cells were located. A lady sitting on the bench in front of the interview room looked up as they approached. She was dressed in a modest grey suit and wore little makeup. It was Bryson's wife.

"Hello. I'm Sergeant Flint. We met the other day." They shook hands. "I would like to have a word with you after we interview your husband."

"Of course." Mrs. Williams sat down. "He didn't do it. Bryson wouldn't hurt a fly."

Flint just nodded and turned away. She had heard it all before. But she did feel a sense of guilt for the woman. She seemed so naive.

After tapping on the door, the detectives entered the room.

Bryson was dressed casually in jeans and a sweatshirt as if he was about to head to the gym. He sure is pleased with himself, Flint thought. *Why isn't he nervous?*

A thin man dressed in a black suit with silver tie sat next to their suspect. He pushed back his chair and stood up when the detectives entered.

"Thank you for taking this interview early." He held out his hand. "Ken Moore. Hope we can clear this misunderstanding quickly, so Mr. Williams can be released."

"Sergeant Flint. And this is Constable Hay." She shook his hand, sat across the table from the lawyer and turned on the recorder. "I take it you have had a chance to speak to your client."

"Yes, of course. He denies any wrongdoing."

"We found what we believe is the weapon used during the commission of a heinous crime on your client's property. The murder of Harris Crest."

"The knife in question was retrieved, if I understand the circumstances, from a burn barrel outside of Mr. Williams's office," Mr. Moore said. "I would like to add that anyone could have tossed the knife there. There is no evidence that it belongs or was used by my client. Furthermore–"

"Let me interrupt you there, Mr. Moore. We have corroborating evidence to back the charge against your client. We have a witness and video that puts Mr. Williams at the crime scene at the time of the murder. The knife has been sent to the crime lab, and we are confident that we will find it is the weapon used to slice at the victim's arms." Flint held up her hand so the lawyer would hear her out before objecting. "And that Mr. Williams's fingerprints will be on the knife."

"Let me begin by saying that this so-called witness and video are both circumstantial evidence. I think you are doing my client a great injustice by arresting him without concrete evidence."

"We can hold Mr. Williams until his bail hearing, and we intend to do that," Flint said in an unnecessarily huffy way. "We have arranged for a hearing to take place tomorrow morning at ten at the courthouse in Nanaimo."

Bryson sat still during the exchange of words that had heated up considerably between his lawyer and the sergeant. Now, he looked up.

Flint felt his gaze on her, even as she sensed the redness creeping up at the back of her neck. How had she let herself get so flustered? Hadn't she laid out a fairly straightforward case showing that Bryson was the guilty party? Although he certainly didn't appear guilty. He sat in his chair, not saying a word, not trembling or unnerved by what was happening. His attitude during questioning wasn't that of a man who had something to hide.

She tried not to show her embarrassment as doubts crowded into her head, troubling ones that lingered and stayed with her when she considered her rush to arrest Bryson. Never mind, she thought. The knife will tell all. He did it. No upper class, blue-blooded, Queen's

University-educated lawyer would save Bryson from his fate.

"Okay, we're finished here," Flint said before Mr. Moore could reply. She closed her notebook and stood up to finalize the conversation.

Hay took her lead, opened the door and spoke to the officer waiting outside. "You can take Mr. Williams back to a holding cell."

Flint stopped at the doorway and turned to Bryson, throwing one last insinuation at him. "Why did you set the cottage on fire? You almost cost one of my officers their life."

When he didn't answer, she strode out of the room. She gave Mrs. Williams a cursory glance before stomping down the hallway. She was too mad to speak to the woman now.

Hay followed in her wake. When they reached the boardroom, he touched the sergeant's arm.

"Are you okay? What was that all about?"

"I know, I know." Flint shook her head. "He just seemed so uninterested. What the hell? He's going to be charged with murder. It's like he's not even... I don't know." She glanced at the constable.

"Don't worry about it. He's our man."

Flint grinned weakly.

Greenwood stood by the whiteboard when they entered the room. She turned at the sound of their chatter.

"Did he confess?"

"No," Flint said, trying not to bark.

"Ryan called and said he won't have anything for us until tomorrow," Greenwood said.

"That's cutting it tight. Bryson will get released if we don't have the evidence."

"Look, boss. Ryan will stay up all night if he has to. You know that," Hay said.

"Yeah, he will," Flint replied. She looked at the updates on the whiteboard, and then at Greenwood. "Good job.

Let's write up our reports and call it an early day. We can't do anything more until we hear from Ryan."

"I'll put on some coffee," Greenwood said.

The sweet smell of java after the stuffy interview was most welcome, as were the sticky cinnamon buns that the constable placed on a plate and set in the centre of the table. The detectives worked for several hours without a break. Hay was the first one to shut down his laptop.

"Done." He stretched his neck from side to side. "Give us a shout after Ryan calls."

"I will," Flint said, pressing her lips into what she hoped was a confident smile.

"All right, then. Tomorrow." Hay pulled on his jacket and left.

"Wait for me," Greenwood shouted after him. She turned to the sergeant. "Go home." She hurried out the door to catch up to Hay.

Flint heard their voices fade as they headed down the long corridor. Then she was left on her own. She pulled out her cell phone and dialled the mayor. Neil didn't answer, so she left him a message to return her call.

The rain had stopped an hour ago, so now the room seemed so quiet. The clock on the opposite wall clunked to the top of the hour.

Flint opened the murder book, flipping back and forth through the pages and mulled over the day. She stared straight ahead mindlessly. After taking another sip of her drink, she pushed the coffee aside and left for home.

* * *

Paulie had given up on finding the treasure. Mia wasn't talking to him anymore. She had found a new job and given notice for the end of the year. He figured it didn't matter, she didn't know any more than she had already told him. Harris may have been her boyfriend, but he had probably just been stringing her along. She was a pretty young thing, and he was way too old for her. It was the only way to keep her interested. Now Paulie wished the waitress had kept her mouth shut about the treasure. It had been a huge waste of time and effort. He chucked the key into the bottom drawer and left for home. On his way out, he spotted Mia in the dining room. She gave him a wry smile. He pursed his lips and gave her a disdainful look. That was all she deserved. He was glad she was quitting the job. Good riddance.

Chapter 22

The ocean had taken on a greyish hue when the fog rolled in early that morning. The tall lighthouse stood on a plinth of rock, its powerful beam breaking through to warn sailors of imminent danger, the ghostly cry of the foghorn a death knell. Flint realized she loved the view from the boardroom. It was a window into the soul of the town. Everything revolved around the castle or the gigantic waves that pounded the shoreline.

The sudden knock on the door sounded like a shot in the night against the sheer quietude of the moment. Flint twirled around and came face to face with the superintendent.

"I heard you arrested someone," Gill said, his smile alarmingly bright. He made himself comfortable in one of the chairs around the table.

"Not exactly. We've detained someone. We're just waiting for the forensics," Flint said as she sat down opposite him.

Gill tilted his head and raised his eyebrows in anticipation.

"For confirmation on the DNA and any fingerprints on the knife."

"Who's the suspect?"

"Bryson Williams," Flint said. "The real estate developer. His newest project is adjacent to the castle."

"Okay. Bryson, you say. That surprises me."

"Really. Every person who turns out to be a killer is your next door neighbour, so to speak," Flint said, trying not to come across as an insufferable know-it-all.

"True enough. Nobody really knows what goes on in a person's head." Gill paused. "But I do know the family fairly well and..."

Flint locked eyes with the superintendent, realizing full well what he was going to say next was just not true. They both knew it. The fire chief who murdered someone the past summer had been his friend. That's why Gill stopped so abruptly, the same thought had just dawned on him. There was a blush on his cheeks. He lowered his head.

"That was a stupid thing to say," Gill finished.

"Anyway I expect to hear from Ryan any moment now," Flint said, trying to change the subject. She desperately needed to get along with the superintendent. Their bad history ran deep, but the success of the team relied on the full cooperation and participation of all its members. She had made good inroads into bridging their differences, but it was a tenuous relationship.

"Give me a shout when you find out." Gill rapped the edge of the table and stood up. "I'll be on my way. I've got a meeting in Victoria at noon. Keep up the good work."

"Thanks. I'll let you know right away."

Flint felt relieved after the superintendent left. He seemed to be in the picture more than ever now. Not that she minded the support, but she hadn't quite mastered her queasiness when she was around that man. It was nothing he did. It's me, not you. She laughed at her profound sense of insecurity.

Moments later, Thornberry strolled into the room and sank into the chair the super had just vacated.

"Any news?"

"Just waiting. Is Jarrett home yet?"

"The hospital is releasing him this afternoon. He'll be fine," Thornberry said. "I just can't stop thinking he could have been killed."

"Yeah. We're all thinking the same thing," Flint said.

Footsteps sounded in the hallway along with a low-pitched whistle.

"Have we got him?" Hay asked as he rounded the corner.

"Not yet."

The constable sat next to Thornberry. "I went to see Jarrett last night. He sure got knocked about by that blast. Bruises all over his face."

Thornberry grimaced and looked out the window. The fog had rolled away, letting the sun warm up the air.

Flint's cell phone pinged as Greenwood sprinted into the room. The sergeant held up her hand to stop the chatter among her team. She nodded her head several times.

"Shit. You're sure?" Flint said.

Her face tensed as she looked down to conceal her disappointment. She placed her phone on the desk and leaned back into her chair. Learning that she had been totally wrong had just taken the wind out of her sails.

"Looks like bad news," Hay said.

"The blood on the knife is Harris's, so we know it's the knife used to attack him." Flint glanced around the faces waiting for the next bit, although she was pretty sure they had already figured it out by the deflated sound of her voice. Even to her own ears, she heard the defeat.

"There was different DNA found in the cracks of the handle. But unfortunately it's not Bryson's. And no clear prints."

"So that's it. We have to let him go?" Greenwood asked.

"I'm afraid so. We're back at square one," Flint said. She really needed to snap out of this and quickly, she thought. So she pressed on. "Okay, everyone. We're not giving up. Let's go over all the evidence one more time."

She expected to get some resistance, but she was wrong. Again.

"I'm on it." Hay grabbed the murder book and opened it to the first page.

"Good. Make it a team effort. Find something," Flint said. "I'll go see the desk sergeant and get Bryson released."

She picked up the phone and made three calls. The first one was to cancel the court date in Nanaimo. The second one was to Bryson's lawyer. She anticipated some pushback from Mr. Moore, but he was polite and thanked her for the courtesy call. The last one was to the front desk sergeant.

Flint left the room and strolled solemnly down the corridor. She couldn't help thinking how Bryson had acted when he was accused of killing Harris. It was said that guilty people yelled and screamed about their rights, but the real estate developer had said nothing. Maybe there was something to it. Because obviously the man was innocent.

The desk sergeant was waiting by the holding area, leaning against the wall, his keys twirling in his fingers. After a short conversation, he handed Flint a large brown envelope with the discharge papers that needed her autograph before he could release Bryson. Once she had signed off, they headed to his cell.

Bryson sat on a thin mattress with his back against the wall, a striped blue and yellow blanket folded neatly at the foot of the bed. A small window set high up on the west wall over his head had evenly spaced bars, spaced so closely that no one would be able to slip through. Sunlight poured in, filtered through the evergreen trees beside the building and into the cell. The light cast a mosaic pattern on the floor by his feet.

Although Bryson had probably heard them approaching, he didn't look up until the door was pulled open.

"How are you doing?" Flint asked.

"I'm fine."

"We don't have any evidence to hold you. You're free to go."

"Okay." Bryson stood up. He ran his hands down his wrinkled jeans and straightened his shirt.

"I'm sorry..." Flint wanted to say more, but it didn't seem the right place or time. "Your lawyer is on his way. He'll give you a ride home."

"And my wife? Has she been told?"

"Mr. Moore said he would call her with the news," Flint said. "The desk sergeant will get you to sign some papers before you leave. Take care."

She walked away but instead of heading to the boardroom where her team was working, she strolled out of the station and hopped into her vehicle. Without hesitation she started up the engine, and then sat back. She needed something. She wasn't sure what it was, but a stiff drink seemed in order although wine was her drink of choice. Regardless, she would have a whisky for a change. With that comforting thought foremost in her mind, she backed up the car and headed home.

Rarely had Flint abandoned her duties so blatantly, but she justified her actions with the text she had just sent to Hay. 'Going home. Call it a day. Meet at eight tomorrow in boardroom.'

With a sigh of relief, Flint pulled into the driveway and turned off the ignition. She could hear shrieks of girlish laughter coming from the backyard. Her daughter. She hadn't phoned ahead to tell them she was coming home early, so when she rounded the corner of the house the screams turned into high-pitched squeals of joy.

"Mommy." Paige fell headlong into the dog as she rushed forward and collapsed into her mother's arms, totally oblivious of the cast on her arm.

"Slow down." Flint gathered Paige against her and held on to her tightly.

It didn't take long for her daughter to wriggle and squirm, trying to pull herself out of the grasp and rush back to her game with the dog.

"She's so independent," Oleane said. "Just like you were at her age."

"I was that bad?" Flint said.

"Worse."

"Is it lunch time yet?"

"We were just going to head inside," Oleane said. "Your dad made some chili."

"Perfect."

"And I picked up a nice sourdough bread at the bakery this morning."

"Even better," Flint said. "I'll go change first."

"Okay." Oleane eyed Flint suspiciously, but she would never ask questions.

Flint took the stairs two at a time, tore off her clothes and jumped into the shower. She leaned on the tile wall, letting the hot water run down her back, and suddenly the day slowed down. All thoughts of that stiff drink went down the drain with the water and suds. Like magic, the connection to life came back just as quickly as it had disappeared. It was seeing her family playing and laughing that always pulled her back from the brink. She had to remember what was most important. With fine memories running through her head, Flint threw on a pair of jeans and a loose sweater. She tied her hair into a long ponytail and headed downstairs.

Her dad stood in front of the stove dishing out the chili into large stoneware bowls. Steam rose off the buttered slices of sourdough bread set in the centre of the table. A shaker of ground hot chili peppers had been placed out of reach of Paige.

Flint took a seat opposite her mom where a full glass of wine had been parked. She took a sip then a big gulp.

After a lively lunch, her dad headed to the living room to read while her mom cleaned up the kitchen.

"I'm going to make some cookies. Why don't you read Paige a story? But hang on a minute." Oleane left the kitchen and came back moments later with a picture book in her hand. "I picked this up yesterday."

"Let me see," Paige said. She clasped onto the new treasure and ran out of the room. A patter of tiny feet sounded as she went up the stairs to her bedroom.

"Thanks, Mom," Flint said and headed upstairs. She stood in the doorway for a minute before entering. Her daughter sat upright in the bed, the book opened to the first page.

"Once upon a time…" Flint began.

After an hour of reading, her daughter's head had fallen onto her shoulder. She reached down and brushed a lock of hair from her eyes. As gently as she could, Flint untangled herself and placed a woolen blanket over the little body.

Flint closed the door behind her quietly and crept down to the kitchen. Her mom gave her a smile as she gathered the dog's leash and her jacket and went out the back entrance. Almost immediately, she lit up a cigarette and blew out the first puff of smoke with a loud exhale. She made her way along the dirt path, under the shelter of the trees to the old steps leading to the waterfront. Bodhi waited for a signal, and then he was off in a flash, diving into the waves, dashing back and forth. He ran so far down the beach, he was a speck in the distance. She could hear the thundering of his paws as he rushed back to her and dropped down in the sand in front of her.

Some days Flint sat on the bottom step and had another smoke. Today she strolled down to the water and walked along the edge for a kilometre or two before turning back. The dog chased gulls as he played in the surf, more than happy to extend the stay.

Everything was hushed when they entered the house. Flint smelled the peanut butter cookies, but her mom wasn't in the kitchen. She fed the dog and went to her room. After a quick refresh of her makeup, minimal though it was, she stared into the mirror. Let's do this, she thought. The meeting with Neil in the restaurant at the castle was set for happy hour, but she feared it wouldn't be happy at all, especially for the mayor. Now she wondered if she had made the right decision. Was breaking up with Neil the right move? Because of the conflict in the case? The mistaken identity that had shaken her world once again. Or was it really because she didn't want a man in her life? One last question lingered in her mind. Would she have regrets? She pulled her eyes away from her reflection and put aside any reservations she had about saving the relationship.

It was still all quiet on the home front. Flint peeked into her daughter's room and saw her playing with her dolls. Her dad had probably fallen asleep in his armchair in front of the fire, his book on his lap. She knew her mom occasionally took an afternoon lie-down since Paige had entered kindergarten in September. A new, horrifying thought struck her, one she had been running from the past few months. There was no denying that her parents were getting older, a reality that made her shudder. She brushed aside that thought and slipped out the back door.

Flint ran her palms along the steering wheel and closed her eyes. She loved this car. She fired up the engine and slowly backed out of the garage and down the driveway. After turning the first corner, she let the Camaro loose. The engine growled as she pressed down on the accelerator. It was a throaty sound that reminded her of freedom, of fun, of memories of her late husband. More thoughts to push away. She headed to the castle road and ripped up the pavement. When she reached the parking lot, she let the car purr softly as she pulled up alongside Neil's truck.

After passing white stick reindeer, flashing stars hanging from the eaves and coloured lights strung up in the trees, Flint drew in a deep breath to muster what was left of her courage and entered the castle. It was all lit up in Christmas cheer, something she was definitely not feeling.

Chapter 23

A continuous low-level hum streamed down from the second floor. Flint stood just inside the doorway. She looked all around, her gaze landing on the large tree, its tiers of lights briefly dazzling her as they blinked off and on in some kind of rhythmic sequence. Underneath the long evergreen boughs were red and silver papered presents, empty probably or maybe for the staff. There was definitely way more glitz than when she had been here the other day with her family.

That particular evening had started out so nice, being surrounded by the ones she cared about the most, and then ended with chaos after the explosion. There was still no compelling explanation for why someone would set the cottage on fire. She was sure the blast was unintentional, but she really didn't give a damn. There had been consequences from someone's careless act. A cottage destroyed. An officer almost killed. When she figured out who the culprit was, she would make them pay for the injury to her constable.

Flint walked through the foyer and stopped in front of the study door. The yellow and black police ribbon was strung up just the same as it had been on the day of the murder, such a contrast to the tinsel trimmings and the cheerful atmosphere that filled the castle. She climbed the stairs, reluctant to confront the mayor now that she was here. The place was packed. The mixture of chatter, laughter and festive music, which had seemed like white noise from below, was almost deafening from where she stood now. She spotted Neil seated by the window. As she made her way over, she nodded to a few people she knew from the town. Paulie dressed in his Sunday best was talking to a man at the far end of the room.

"You look great." Neil stood up. He was dressed in blue woollen slacks and a crisp white shirt without a tie. His brown hair was trimmed shorter than normal. His soft brown eyes had a hint of sadness in them.

"Thanks," Flint said. She sat down and rested her hands in her lap.

"Did you drive the Camaro tonight?"

"Yes. I love that car," Flint said.

Neil rearranged the silverware beside his plate, a habit she had seen before when he was on edge. The motion drew her eyes to the small box covered in gold wrapping paper beside his wine glass. She pulled her gaze away.

"I thought we could share a bottle of wine," Neil said.

"Sure, sounds nice."

"Your choice." He beckoned the waitress over.

"Hello. I'll be your server for the evening," Mia said. She looked at the sergeant. "Oh, sorry, I didn't recognize you at first. My mind is all over the place tonight."

"Hi, Mia," Flint said. She opened the menu and glanced down the list of wines. "So I'm supposed to pick the wine for tonight."

"Do you want the same as the other night?" Mia asked.

"No. We always get the most expensive bottle when my dad is paying."

"You guys are bad. But cost is no object tonight," Neil said, trying to keep the mood light.

"How about something from the Naramata Bench?" Flint asked.

"The Lake Breeze has a nice Pinot Noir," Mia said.

"Perfect."

"And could we have a charcuterie board, as well?" Neil asked.

"Of course. I won't be a moment."

Flint watched as Mia meandered through the tables and disappeared into the kitchen.

They sat there, neither of them talking about things that mattered, keeping the conversation going with an occasional pause of silence until the waitress returned. Mia moved the water glasses and placed the platter of cheese, crackers and deli meats between the plates.

"I'll do the honours," Neil said as he reached for the bottle of wine.

"Enjoy. Is there anything else I can get you?" Mia asked.

"No, thank you. We're good, I think," Neil said.

Flint sipped her wine and nibbled on the food as Neil chatted about the sailboat he was working on. He had a strong baritone voice that was smooth and soothing. His enthusiasm for his undertaking was contagious. She found herself shedding her doubts about him, about them.

"That sounds incredible," Flint said and selected another cheese.

"So what do you think?" Neil asked. "Should we go for a spin through the posh neighbourhoods and see the light displays? See how the other half lives."

"Oh, I think we're doing okay in life," Flint said and finished off her wine. "Let's do it."

They strolled along the pathway to the parking lot, stopping in front of the Camaro. Neil took both her hands into his. Flint leaned in. She could feel his warm breath against her cheek. He pulled her in. It was the perfect kiss.

The cry was clear in the crisp air. It was hard to distinguish whether the sound had come from a human or an injured gull. They pivoted toward the direction of the noise.

A girl running toward them zigzagged between the vehicles. In her haste, she stumbled on the loose gravel and landed on her knees. She picked herself up and sobbed uncontrollably. Her lips quivered, and her eyes swelled with tears.

"It's Mia," Flint said and rushed to the waitress's side. "Are you okay? What happened?" She drew the girl into her arms until the sobbing subsided to light hiccups that soon grew quiet.

"He just fired me. Just like that," Mia said. "He can't do that, can he? I need every penny I make."

"Here. Sit down." Flint pulled her over and opened the car door. "Tell us how this happened."

"He followed me to the ladies' room and pushed me against the wall. I thought he was going to hurt me. He screamed at me, called me a lying bitch. He's gone mad."

"Do you mean Paulie?"

"Yeah. He said I lied to him about the key and—" Mia suddenly stopped speaking and went to stand up as if to escape.

"Mia. What key are you talking about?" Flint held her ground and placed her hand on the top of the door, blocking her exit.

The girl pushed back into the seat, tilted her head back and closed her eyes.

"Mia?"

"The key in the time capsule."

Flint glanced sideways at Neil.

"Who has the key?" she asked.

"Paulie."

"How did he get it?"

"I'm not sure," Mia said.

"You'll have to do better than that," Flint said. "Let's start from the beginning."

"Okay. So, like, Harris was my boyfriend…"

"What? You didn't think that was something you should have told me?" Flint asked.

Mia didn't answer.

"Okay. Go on," Flint said, holding back her annoyance.

"Sorry. I guess I should have. Anyway Harris told me about some key. I told Paulie about it." Mia looked down at the ground. "I guess I wanted him to think I was cool or something. That was stupid. He's been hounding me since."

"I'm not quite following you," Flint said.

"Harris read his mom's diary," Mia said. "Look. There was nothing wrong with doing that. She died."

"Okay."

"So anyway, it was all there. The thing about the key unlocking a treasure. So Harris had to dig up the capsule to get the key."

"Did Paulie kill Harris?"

"Oh, shit. I never thought about that," Mia said. She swallowed hard. "Is he going to kill me, do you think?"

"No." Although Flint wasn't sure what the score was at this point.

"Okay." Mia plucked at her lips. "Maybe Paulie took the key when he went into the study. You know, after Harris was already dead." She stopped. "That means he didn't kill Harris. And he won't hurt me? Right?" She shuddered and pulled her jacket in closer.

"So all of that doesn't explain why Paulie fired you tonight. What did you lie to him about?"

"Nothing."

Flint waited.

"He couldn't figure out what the key unlocked until tonight. Then he remembered I'd said something about wine that had been left in the original cellar. He was trying to say that I knew all along where the treasure would be and I was just a bitch for not telling him. But that's not true. I didn't know."

"But you do now?" Flint asked.

"Yeah. He told me when we were in the washroom," Mia said. Tears rolled down her cheeks.

"What did Paulie tell you?"

"He said there was no doubt in his mind that there was a jib door in the old cellar. They had built concealed doors that blended into the wall for centuries in European castles. Why not here in this castle? He had missed it the first time round, but now he knew what he was looking for, and he would be damned if he would let me stand in his way. Then, he pushed me harder against the wall and left. Why is he blaming me for all of this?"

"Is Paulie there now?" Flint asked.

"I think so."

Flint pulled out her cell phone and called for backup.

"What should I do?" Mia asked.

"You stay here. Do you hear me?"

"Yeah, okay," Mia sobbed.

"Come with me, Neil," Flint said. She started to sprint away, and then stopped abruptly. "Mia. I don't know where the old cellar is. Do you?"

"Yeah."

"Hurry up," Flint shouted.

"I'm coming." Mia jumped out of the vehicle, slamming the door behind her.

The three of them dashed across the parking lot. When they reached the end of the pathway, Mia steered them along the side of the building to an oak door recessed into the stone.

"It's down there," Mia said.

"Wait here. Don't come down," Flint said. "Neil, stay behind me but not too close. We don't know what state of mind Paulie is in. He could pose a threat."

"Okay."

Flint reached under her jacket and drew out her Smith & Wesson from its holster, glad she was never without it.

Mia's eyes opened wide at the sight of the weapon.

"Ready?" Flint asked.

She gave the door a little shove. It swung slowly inward. A narrow set of stairs leading down smelled of mold and dampness. The wood creaked when Flint placed a foot on the first step, her heart stuck in her throat. Please, please, she thought as the darkness crowded in around her. The fear was always there, to be conquered over and over again. She took another step, aware of the slippery feeling under her shoe, holding her gun tight against her body. She took the next step, and then the next until she landed on a rough surface of chiselled rock covered in a slimy, green algae. Up ahead, a dim light shone from a gap in the wall.

The sergeant crept forward quietly, extending her arms out front, her trigger finger along the frame of the gun. When she had almost reached the opening, a loud crash sounded followed by a slew of swearing.

"Shit. God damn it." The words bounced and reverberated against the rock walls.

Flint froze. She turned her head slightly to the right and held up a closed fist to Neil.

He stopped moving and held his breath.

Flint stepped forward, her gun pointed straight at a figure kneeling on the floor. The man twisted around at the scuffle of her shoes.

"Police. Stand up. Hands over your head."

Flint heard the clatter of the key as it hit the floor.

Chapter 24

"That bloody bitch," Paulie shouted.

Pounding footfalls sounded behind the sergeant.

"Turn around," Flint said to the manager.

There was a shuffle of boots, and Hay rounded the corner.

"Why? I haven't done anything wrong." Paulie backed up.

"We'll start with theft, and if you don't get moving, I'll add resisting arrest." Flint holstered her gun. "Constable, cuff the man."

Paulie turned away and placed his hands behind him.

Hay slapped on the cuffs and jerked him forward with a rough tug on his arms.

"Hey, take it easy."

"Move it."

When they stepped across the threshold into the night, several police cruisers were angled across the doorway, their lights flashing across the crowd that had gathered.

Hay strode over to his vehicle and placed Paulie into the back seat. With a blast of the siren, he cleared a path through the onlookers and drove screaming down the castle road to the station.

"Thornberry. Where the hell are you? Get your ass down here right now," Flint shouted when the corporal didn't answer and the recording started. She pushed her cell phone back into her pocket.

"Are you yelling at me?" Thornberry asked as she came up behind the sergeant.

"Yeah, sorry. This is so messed up," Flint said. "Guard this door with your life. I'll be right back."

"You got it."

Flint searched for Mia and Neil among the people still standing around. She found them sitting on the steps at the front entrance. The mayor had flung his coat over the waitress's shoulders. Her mascara had made black streaks down her cheeks, and her eyes were swollen red.

"Thanks for all your help. Do you think you can take Mia home?"

"Of course." Neil jumped up.

"What about my job?" Mia asked.

"We'll sort that out tomorrow when you come into the station," Flint said.

"Why do I have to do that?"

"You held back vital information that could have been useful in our investigation," Flint said.

"I'm sorry. I didn't realize..." Mia brushed away a tear with an annoyed sweep of her hand. "I honestly thought it was just a joke Harris was playing."

"Tomorrow. Get some rest." The sergeant's jaw clenched and unclenched, holding back more harsh words.

Flint rushed back to the corporal who stood at the cellar doorway stamping her feet to ward off the cold.

"Shit, it's cold out here."

"Follow me," Flint said.

She ran her hand along the inner wall and found the light switch. The florescent lamp hummed loudly before it blinked on. The cellar looked even creepier in the bright light. This time she clasped the handrail as she headed down the stairs.

"Watch your step. It's super slippery."

"What's down here?" Thornberry asked as she lost her footing and let out a yelp.

"Not sure yet."

Flint crossed over to the opening and entered the low-ceilinged room. She looked down on the floor at a broken bottle, its red contents seeped into the cracks of the rock like a pool of blood. It was a 1930s vintage from France.

"There's grand theft right there," Flint muttered.

Thornberry nodded and glanced around the space.

There were several hand-wrought steel wine racks filled with dusty bottles at the back of the tiny room. The bottles from one of the smaller racks had been removed, and the whole thing was pushed aside, revealing an opening in the wall. It appeared to be a cubby hole. The door itself blended with the surrounding wall, with a lock in the middle that was barely visible. The hidden door would have been indiscernible to the casual onlooker.

Flint picked up the key that lay on the floor where it had fallen and placed it in her pocket. Then she flashed her torch into the opening.

"We've got something," the sergeant said and reached into the cupboard. Her fingers touched a cold metal object. She dragged it out of the deep recess, placed it on the floor and sat back on her heels. "What do you think is in it?"

"Looks like a treasure chest to me," Thornberry said.

"Here goes." Flint lifted the lid.

Both detectives leaned in.

"It's just an envelope," Thornberry said. "Are the diamonds underneath?"

"Could be bearer bonds or something like that in here," Flint said as she picked up the brown packet. There was nothing else in the box. She tilted the envelope and let the contents spill out.

"What is it?"

Flint stood up, staring at the official document that she held in her hand.

"Oh my God. This is nuts," she said.

"What? Let me see," Thornberry said. She looked over the sergeant's shoulder and read. "Holy shit. Is this for real?"

Flint flipped the document front to back and back again. "Yeah, I believe it is."

"We have to go tell him right away."

"Who?" Flint tapped the paper with her finger. "Him or Charles?"

"Ah. Both, I guess," Thornberry said.

"Okay. Let's go." Flint picked up the box and tucked it under her arm.

"So is this what the whole thing has been about?" Thornberry asked.

Flint didn't have an answer for that, so she climbed the steps in silence. There was police tape strung across the entrance as they left the cellar.

"Someone is quite enthusiastic," Flint said as she crawled under the tape and shut the door.

The crowds had dispersed as quickly as they had arrived. It was too cold to hang out when all the action stopped. The solitary police cruiser still on the scene had two officers chatting inside, engine running and heater on full blast.

Flint tapped on the driver's side roof. The officer rolled down the window just a crack. "Hello, Sergeant. What can we do for you?" He smiled.

"Stay until forensics get here."

"Sure thing," the officers said. "Ryan said he'll be here within the hour."

"Great. Thanks, guys." She rapped on the hood and walked away.

Flint and Thornberry rounded the corner, strolled past the fountain and headed to the cottages. As they topped the ridge, they could see wisps of purplish smoke curling out of the chimney stack at Charles's place.

The burnt-out shell of the cottage next door filled Flint's nostrils with a rank stench. She shuddered thinking about Jarrett and his close call, how bad it could have been. A peal of laughter made her look over to a group of kids hanging out in a tight circle. They were standing near the pathway that cut through the woods to Bryson's property.

"What's going on over there?" Flint asked. She caught a whiff of the pungent smell of marijuana wafting through the air.

"I have no idea, but that's pot they're smoking," Thornberry said as she wrinkled her nose.

"Let's go over and see what they're up to," Flint said as she trudged the rest of the way down the hill.

The kids pulled out of their circle as the detectives walked up to them. A short, stocky kid with a bad complexion chucked something on the ground.

"Why are you guys hanging around smoking next to the house that just burnt down?" Flint asked.

"I'm just waiting for my dad," a tall kid said. He brushed back his hair with a sweep of his hand.

"Who's that?"

"The doctor. He's in with the old man."

"Do you mean Dr. Lane is your dad?"

"Yeah."

"What's your name?"

"Shawn."

"Okay. What about the rest of you guys?" Flint asked.

"We're not doing anything wrong," the stocky kid said. He kicked at the dirt with his boots. "I'm out of here."

"Hang on a second," Flint said. "We're going to need your names and addresses."

"No way."

"Would you rather I haul the lot of you into the station right now?" Flint asked. "We are looking for the person responsible for burning down that cottage." She turned to Thornberry. "Get their info."

"I'm going to report you for hassling us," a thin kid named Robert said.

"Yeah, yeah," Thornberry said. After getting all their names jotted into her notebook, she closed it and stuck it in her pocket.

"Let's go." Flint turned away and walked back up the path.

"Do you think one of them started the fire?" Thornberry asked.

"We'll definitely look into it," Flint said. "Maybe they were in it together."

"I don't like that one kid," Thornberry said. "Jim."

"Could be trouble."

Flint stepped up to the door at Charles's place and knocked lightly.

"Come in," someone shouted, and then the door swung open.

Flint stepped inside, Thornberry right behind her. She stopped suddenly, surprised at the number of people in the room.

"Shut the door. It's cold out there. Bad for the patient," Dr. Chester Lane said.

"I'm not a patient, you fool," Charles said. "It was just a little case of nerves. Stop fussing."

"Here, take my seat. I'm just headed out." Bryson stood up.

"No, wait. What I have to say concerns you," Flint said.

"Really? I thought we'd been through everything. Take my seat anyway." He remained standing.

"I think you're going to need to be sitting down to hear this," Flint said. "Don't worry, it's nothing to do with the investigation."

Bryson frowned and plopped back into the chair.

"Does this concern me or should I go?" Dr. Lane asked. "My son is outside waiting for me."

"I think you should stay, too."

"All right." The doctor walked over to the fireplace and added another log, stoking it until it caught. The flames crackled in the silence.

"What have you got there?" Charles asked, pointing to the box that was still tucked under the sergeant's arm.

"Right." Flint pulled up a chair at the kitchen table and set the metal container down. "I'm not sure how to begin."

"Just spit it out," Charles said.

Flint glanced at Thornberry who had positioned herself beside the old man, just in case.

"I recognize that box." Charles leaned forward.

"And what about the name Allison Williams?" Flint said and looked around the room.

"That's my mom. What the hell is going on?" Bryson asked. He perched on the edge of his chair.

"Hang on there, Bryson," Flint said. She turned to Charles. "Did you know Miss Williams?"

"Of course. She was the primary school teacher." He rolled his hand over his mouth.

"She died a few years ago," Bryson said. "I don't understand what she has to do with anything. Why are you interested in my mom?"

"Your wife knew her, as well?" Flint asked, ignoring Bryson for the moment.

"They were best friends," Charles said.

"Let me explain where I got this." She removed the document from the box and put it on the table.

"What is it?" Bryson asked.

"Just listen," Flint said and held up her hand.

Dr. Lane sat back in his chair and crossed his arms.

"I'll start from the beginning. There was a key in the time capsule. I believe your wife put it there," Flint said.

Charles nodded in agreement. "I always thought she was up to something."

"The key fits into a hidden door in the old wine cellar. A jib door. We found this in the cubby hole." Flint tapped the box. "We opened it up just a little while ago and found a birth certificate. There's a seal at the top. I'm certain it's authentic." She paused. "I don't know why your wife hid the document knowing it wouldn't be found until after she died, and I suppose you as well."

Charles lowered his head while he listened to the sergeant.

"Do you know who was named as the father?" Flint asked.

"I guess you're telling us now," Charles said.

Flint nodded.

"What the hell does that mean?" Bryson asked. "What father? The father of who?"

"Give me another moment. I'm coming to the end of it."

Bryson was about to say more, but the look the sergeant gave him made him stop.

"Did you know your wife had found out the truth?" Flint continued.

"I didn't know the truth until now," Charles said.

"Okay. But you must have suspected it. Really? How could you not?"

"Sure, I suspected, but I didn't know."

"And your wife?" Flint asked again.

"Like I said, Allison and she were best friends. And when you spend a lot of time with someone, you kind of figure things out. And my wife always went one step further. She would have looked for proof."

"Why do you think she didn't confront you about it?"

"Because I'm a rogue, and she was an angel."

"Okay. But why would she leave the document to be found in the future? I don't quite get that part."

"That one's easy. She wouldn't want the child to be cheated of his legacy."

"Okay. Could someone put me in the loop? I have no idea what you guys are talking about. So who's this child?" Bryson asked. "It sounds like you're telling me I have a brother somewhere my mother kept from me? That's crazy."

"Well, it appears you are," Charles said.

"I'm what? I'm totally lost now." Bryson threw his hands up.

"You're the child," Flint said. "There is no brother."

"Could someone explain?" Bryson looked from Flint to Charles.

"I had an affair with Allison early in my marriage," Charles said.

"Oh, Jesus," Bryson said.

"We broke it off after only a few months. I knew that she had a child. You, apparently. But Allison never contacted me, so I let it go. I swear, I didn't know you were mine. I should have tried to find out. Why did she keep it from me?" He placed his head in his hands.

The room was silent. Flint watched Bryson to see which way he would go, but he just stared into the fireplace.

"Here I am blaming Allison. I guess I'm just a coward for not taking some action myself," Charles said. "I'm sorry. You must hate me."

"Why should I hate you? I'm stunned. I don't know what to say," Bryson said. He sat back in his chair.

Flint sat still, hoping the situation wouldn't turn ugly.

"My mom said my dad died in a motorcycle accident before I was born." Bryson slapped his forehead. "Wow, my mom lied to me. She lied to both of us."

Thornberry fidgeted on her feet.

The old man had turned pale.

"Look. We're good friends, Charles. We have been friends for quite a while." Bryson looked around the room. "My mom must have had a good reason for keeping me in the dark. Maybe she was ashamed."

"I should be the one who is ashamed. For what I did. I let down both women," Charles said.

"No. That's not right. You didn't know."

"Maybe not, but I cheated on my wife. And your mother too."

Bryson nodded.

"What should we do?" Charles asked.

"Nothing's really changed for me." Bryson looked at the old man. "I guess what I'm saying is that I'm okay with this if you are."

"So you forgive me?"

"Hell, yeah." Bryson burst out laughing.

"Yeah. You're okay with it?" Charles's hands were shaking.

"Maybe it was fate that we became friends." Bryson shook his head.

"Drinks all round?" Dr. Lane asked.

"Yes, yes. This is a great day," Charles said as tears rolled down his cheeks. "I thought I had lost everything, but now..."

"Take it easy," Dr. Lane said.

"Oh, stop fussing. Just get me a drink." Charles waved his hand at the doctor. "Thank you, Sergeant."

"No problem," Flint said. "I'm glad this worked out for everyone." She stood up and gestured to the corporal. "We'll be on our way now. Take care."

"I'll walk up the hill with you," Dr. Lane said. "Call me if you need anything, Charles." He smiled at the old man.

"I'm fine," Charles said. "Throw on another log there, Bryson. We have some things to talk about."

"Sure."

Flint looked back before closing the door. Bryson stood by his dad's chair with his hand on his shoulder. Not quite a hug but close. Dr. Lane walked beside the detectives as they headed up the slope.

"Did you know, Dr. Lane?" Flint asked.

"No. I'm speechless."

"Hey, Dad. Wait up." Shawn rushed up to them.

Flint glanced back to the woods, but everyone had disappeared.

"I don't know if you've met my son. Shawn."

"Yes as a matter of fact, we met earlier."

Shawn glanced at the sergeant.

"Oh, really? Where was that?"

"He was hanging around with a bunch of kids on the pathway on the other side of the cottage. By the woods."

"I see," Dr. Lane said. "He wasn't getting into any trouble. Was he?"

"Not that we know of," Flint said.

"Was your girlfriend with you?" The doctor turned to his son and gave him a light punch on the arm.

"See you at the truck," Shawn said and sprinted away up the hill.

"Okay," Dr. Lane said and shrugged. "Boys. They're more trouble than girls."

"Maybe. Who's his girlfriend?"

"Janice. She has a job as apprentice gardener at the castle."

"Oh," Flint said and glanced sideways at Thornberry. "So do you know these kids your son hangs out with?"

"Yeah, mostly."

"What about the stocky kid, Jim? Jim Heron, I think?"

"That's right," Thornberry said.

"He's new in town. I am a bit wary of him."

"Why's that?"

"I think he's the one who supplies them the pot they smoke," Dr. Lane said. "I don't think Shawn smoked before they met up."

"So you know about that?"

"Yes, yes. I know what goes on. I try to keep my eye on him so things don't get out of hand."

"Good idea," Flint said.

When they reached the parking lot, Shawn was standing by his dad's vehicle. He had his cell phone in his hand, his fingers rapidly skimming over the screen.

"Talk to you later, Dr. Lane," Flint said.

"Sure thing." He hopped into his car and they sped off.

"I was thinking it's time we had another chat with Janice Jenkins," Flint said and leaned against her vehicle.

"I think you're right," Thornberry said. "She's not telling us everything."

"Get Hay to bring her into the station first thing in the morning."

"You bet," Thornberry said.

"So Bryson and Charles. That was the weirdest thing I've ever seen," Flint said.

"No kidding." Thornberry paused. "You know something even weirder?"

"What's that?"

"If Harris hadn't dug up the capsule early those two would never have found each other."

"You're right. Life is strange. You never know where it's going to lead you," Flint said.

"There's that. Now Charles and Bryson have each other," Thornberry said.

"We like happy endings." Flint smiled and got into the Camaro. She put her key into the ignition and fired it up. The deep, resonant sound of the engine was music to her ears. She left a spray of gravel behind as she roared out of the lot.

Thornberry watched the tail-lights disappear and listened to the drone of the muffler fade as the sergeant booted it down the hill.

Chapter 25

A high-pressure ridge had settled over the island overnight, bringing with it a flawless sky, pure and cloudless. So the cold weather was here to stay for a few days more, Flint thought. She shivered and looked out the bedroom window. The ocean was calm, barely a ripple on its surface. She lingered for a few minutes more, watching the gulls swooping on the invisible thermals and thinking about the evening before with Neil. The box he had given her contained a beautiful gold locket. She fingered the chain around her neck and sighed.

A page had been turned in her life. She had taken a very shallow approach to relationships over the last few months. Last night changed all that. She was certain she was doomed to pick the wrong man over and over. It would be easier just to leave them out of her life. But with everything that had happened, pushing him away, even pointing an accusatory finger at him for being the killer, Neil had remained kind and supportive. He had proved that good men were alive and well.

Today she felt a greater certainty about her choices being right, not only about romantic partners, but also about friends. She realized she was not an island but a part of the community with connections that she valued.

Flint hummed to herself as she got ready. It would be another trying day, but she didn't feel so alone anymore. She tiptoed down the stairs, gave the dog a quick pat on the head and went out the back door.

Flint sat at her desk with the lights on low. She put her feet up on the desk, leaned back into her chair and closed her eyes. Her light snooze was interrupted by an ear-piercing ring. She bolted upright, pulling her legs off the desk, almost tipping her chair over in the effort and grabbed the phone. She spoke to Ryan for several minutes. After hanging up, she mulled over what he had said. She hadn't been surprised that Paulie's DNA wasn't a match. He was a lot of things, but a murderer wasn't one of them. Just a greedy bastard and quite possibly the biggest ass she had ever met. The forensic scientist had nothing from the cellar but that was a moot point.

Flint picked up the phone and called through to the desk sergeant.

"You can release Paulie Webb. I'm not charging him with anything at this moment," Flint said. "You can tell him there may be charges pending. That's all you need to say."

"Okay, boss. Will do."

Flint sat back and thought about it. She couldn't let Paulie get away with his bad behaviour, so at the very least she would charge him with impeding the investigation. And the way he had treated Mia desired some attention. Maybe assault. She looked at her watch. The team would be in soon, so she headed to the boardroom.

Thornberry and Greenwood walked into the room together and sat down.

"Where's Hay?" Flint asked.

"He just brought Janice in," Thornberry said. "They're waiting for you in the interview room."

"All right." Flint looked at the detectives. "You two can keep yourselves busy with updating your reports."

"Oh, all the fun stuff," Thornberry said.

"I don't mind." Greenwood snickered.

"After a few years, you will," Thornberry said and jabbed at the constable's arm.

"Try to get along," Flint said as she walked out.

Hay waited on a bench. He had his phone in his hand.

"Are you ready?" she said.

"Sure. That was Jarrett. He's coming in this afternoon."

"What's up?"

"I don't know."

Flint glared at him. She had a pretty good idea, as well.

The gardener was slumped in her chair when the detectives entered the room.

"Hello, Janice," Flint said. "I'm Sergeant Flint."

"Yeah, I know."

"We want to follow up on some questions," Flint said as she sat opposite the girl.

"I guess. This won't take long, I hope. I have to get to work."

"No, it won't take long." Flint pushed on the recorder, stated the time and day and who was in the room. Then she looked at Janice. "Do you want a lawyer present?"

"What? No. I thought you just wanted to ask me some stuff."

"Okay, that's fine. Let's carry on." Flint opened her notepad. "I think you haven't been quite honest about who was in the study the morning of the ceremony?"

"I didn't see anything."

"I think you heard who Harris was talking to," Flint said. She placed her elbows on the table and leaned forward. "The window was open, and the door was ajar."

Janice glanced over to Hay and back to the sergeant. "I heard someone."

Flint kept her gaze steady and waited.

"Okay. It was the doctor."

"Do you mean Dr. Lane?"

"Yes."

"Did you hear what was said?"

"They were arguing about someone."

"Did you catch the name?"

"I think it was John."

Flint glanced at the constable. Hay shrugged. Who the hell was John?

"Okay. Why didn't you tell us this before?"

"I didn't want him to get into any trouble. He's Shawn's dad..." She faded off.

"I see. And Shawn is your boyfriend?"

"I guess. Yeah."

"Do you know who this John guy is?"

"No."

"Okay. Is there anything else you can tell us?" Flint asked.

"No. I don't think so."

"It would be wise for you to speak up now," Flint said.

"No, I don't know anything else."

"Okay." Flint pushed the recorder off and handed Janice her card. "If you remember anything else the men said, call me."

"Okay."

"Hay will give you a ride to work."

"Thanks." Janice pushed her chair away, scraping the legs against the floor.

"I'll be right back," Hay said.

"Okay. I'll give you a shout when we locate the good doctor," Flint said. "You can pick him up on the way back, hopefully."

Hay nodded, the chagrined expression on his face spoke volumes.

Flint felt the same. It would be bad if the doctor was the killer. She headed back to the boardroom where the detectives had their noses in their laptops. They both looked up when she entered the room.

"What did the gardener say?" Thornberry asked.

"She said the doctor was in the study arguing with Harris on the day of the ceremony."

"Oh, shit. Really."

"I'll phone to his practice and see if he's there. Hay will bring him into the station." Flint plopped down into her chair.

"She could be wrong," Greenwood said.

Flint nodded and picked up the phone. After the call, she stood up and walked over to the window. The castle sparkled in the sunlight. She would prefer to have the criminal element involved in these sorts of crimes not the pillars of the community. What was happening in her town? She snorted a laugh. Criminal elements? Really. There were no boundary lines for murder. She texted Hay the address for Dr. Lane. It would be at least an hour before he returned to the station, so she opened up the murder book and checked a few things.

There was a calmness inside the room, the same as the quiet of the ocean that morning. But the anxiety Flint felt coursing through her body was anything but pleasant. She hid it well from the others by diving into her work. A glance at the others made her think they were probably feeling the same. She flipped the page and jotted down a question to ask at the interview.

Her cell phone pinged. Flint looked at the screen.

"Showtime." Flint got up and left. When she opened the door, Dr. Lane sat with his hands on his lap and head down. She took a chair beside Hay, opposite the doctor.

"Thank you for coming. We have a few questions for you. I would suggest that you might want to have a lawyer present."

"No, I'm good. I'm happy to help," Dr. Lane said.

"Okay." Flint turned on the recorder. She studied the doctor for a minute before speaking. "We have a witness who heard you arguing with the victim on the day of the ceremony. With Harris."

Dr. Lane leaned forward, his elbows on the table and hands clasped. "Look. I was there, but I left Harris alive and well."

"Really? And why would you not tell us this earlier? There have been a lot of people not coming forward with the truth, and it has really slowed down my investigation. Of all people, you should know better."

"Sorry. You're right. But I didn't want to muddy the waters." He frowned. "It was just Harris trying to goad me."

"In what way? Can you explain?"

"Well, did you know Harris had an older brother that drowned?"

"John?" Flint guessed.

"Yeah."

"Go on."

"I can't remember what year it was, maybe 1983. I was in my second year at university. Anyway, John and I were good buddies. One weekend I came back here and we met up. We took our boards up the coast to catch some bigger waves. I was on my fourth wave in and waited for him on the shore. But John didn't make it back in alive. When his body washed ashore, the coroner examined him and figured he had hit his head on his board and drowned."

Flint looked at Hay, not sure where this was going. She kept quiet and let him continue with his story. Maybe all the dots would connect.

"I was devastated. Everyone was," Dr. Lane said. "Harris was only, I don't know, three or four years old. He probably didn't even remember his brother all that well. But after his mom died a few months ago, he got a hold of his mother's journals. And that's where he found out about how John had died. Neither parent had ever said anything to him, so he didn't know his brother had drowned. I guess he must have thought all this time that it was natural causes or some disease or something." He shrugged. "Anyway, Harris called me up that morning and said he had something important to tell me. I thought it was something to do with his dad, so I went straight over there. He threatened to tell everyone that I was responsible for his brother's death. That he drowned because I didn't save him. Which was nonsense. Anyway, he said unless I helped him stop Bryson from developing his land, he would tell everyone what I did. He said there was proof in his mother's journal. He kept shouting at me that I could stop Bryson. At that point, I just laughed at him. I guess Harris thought I could do something because I'm on the land development advisory committee." He took a deep breath. "I told him I didn't care if he wanted to spread rumours. The drowning was an accident. And to be honest, I really couldn't see how anybody could stop the development anyway. I tried to reason with Harris, but he wasn't having it, so I left."

"That's a hell of a story," Flint said.

"Yeah."

"Okay, I want to believe you." Flint tugged at her bottom lip. "I think the best way to clear this up is to take a blood sample and send it off to the lab."

"I'm okay with that," Dr. Lane said and stood up. "So if that's it, I have patients waiting."

"Look. I'm going to have to hold you overnight," Flint said. "Until the results come back."

"Seriously?"

"Yeah. I think you better call your lawyer now." Flint tilted her chin at Hay.

The constable pushed his chair back. "Sorry, doc. Protocol."

"Oh, boy. Could you call Shawn for me?" Dr. Lane gazed at the sergeant.

"I will."

∗ ∗ ∗

Flint sat in her chair for a few minutes after the two men left the room. She thought about the knife. And the sequence of events. The fire. The explosion. Was the doctor a smoker? She didn't think so, although most people didn't know she smoked. But the two events were most likely unrelated. She had always had it in the back of her mind that the fire had nothing to do with the murder. The decisive factor was the blood on the knife. It was time to send everybody home for the night, so she headed back to the boardroom.

After the team left, Flint stood by the window and looked at the castle in the distance. She wondered if Ryan was still in the building. A quick call told her that he was, so she locked up and walked down the hallway to see him.

Flint could hear jazz music coming from under the door. She knocked lightly and entered the room. It was a comfortable space with framed photos of mountain scenery hung on the muted green walls. The view from his window was the same one she enjoyed from her office. Ryan sat at his desk with several folders opened. He reached behind him and shut off the radio.

"It's going to be another long night." He held up the blood sample from the doctor.

"Do you mind? I know it's a lot to ask, but I hate seeing the doctor sitting in that cell." She paused. "The quicker we can make a determination of his innocence or guilt the better."

"I agree. I was actually out the door to the lab in Nanaimo when you called."

"Call me when you get the results."

"Even if it's in the middle of the night?"

"I probably won't be able to sleep anyway. So yeah. Call me," Flint said. She touched his arm and squeezed it gently. "I don't know how I will be able to repay you for all these all-nighters."

"I have a few ideas," Ryan said.

"You're a bum." Flint punched his shoulder. She watched him sprint to the front entryway and heard the door slam.

"I don't feel good about this," Flint murmured and left the station.

Chapter 26

Flint lay on top of the covers, propped up with several pillows and one under her knees. She put her book down on her lap and took a sip of her hot chocolate. The green numbers on her alarm clock read three twenty-five. Last time she looked, it said three fifteen. She couldn't concentrate on the words on the page. She hadn't even gotten through one chapter, in what, over four hours. Everything floated around in her head but not in any ordered way. She didn't want the doctor to be the person responsible for what had happened to Harris, but where did she go from here if it wasn't him? There were no other leads.

The light flickered, once, then twice and stayed on. The wind had picked up a few hours ago and now roared across the ocean, pounding the coast with a mighty fist. The weather front had broken down quicker than usual and stalled over the other side of the island. Heavy rains would follow by morning. Every major crime investigation seemed to slow down, then break loose the same way. She hoped that would happen again. She stretched her back and dropped her legs over the edge of the bed. As she crept down the stairs, her cell phone pinged but she didn't hear it.

After making another drink, Flint headed back to her room. She sat in the alcove and listened to the wind as it whistled through the trees. It was still early, but she couldn't just sit here any longer and wait. She had a hot shower and got dressed. When she entered the kitchen, she was surprised to see her dad sitting at the table with a mug cupped in his hands.

"I couldn't sleep either. I'm getting old," Victor said.

He gazed at his daughter. The expression Flint wore was calm, except for the spooked look in her eyes.

"You cracked the case," he said.

"We're close. We'll talk later," Flint said.

"Okay, sweetheart."

The streets were dark and empty. Halfway to the station it began to rain, first with large drops, and then a curtain that made visibility almost non-existent.

On arrival, Flint headed straight to her office and fired up her laptop. After downloading her emails, she glanced at her phone and realized Ryan had called over an hour and a half ago. She rushed down the hallway, knowing he would be back in his office writing up his report.

Flint knocked on his door and entered.

"Sorry, I missed your call," Flint said.

"No problem."

Flint waited for the forensic scientist to continue. She took a seat.

"It's been a bitch," Ryan said. "I got one of the other guys to come in and help."

"Okay."

"I thought I got it wrong, but Paul confirmed it. It's really bad news, I'm afraid."

"How bad?"

"Only half of the markers matched."

"We can't use that?"

"It's not Dr. Lane's DNA, Flint. But the close match to the DNA on the knife strongly suggests the DNA is from a child or possibly a sibling of the doctor's."

"Oh, shit. You mean Shawn, don't you?" Flint asked.

"Yes. Unless the doctor has another son or a brother. But I don't think he does."

"Shawn is an only child, as is his father." Flint paused. "And no possibility of it being a mistake?" She didn't want to say that, but she also needed to know it was an absolute.

"You know, you always ask the hard question, Flint," Ryan said. "So yeah, I ran it again. There's no mistake. But to be clear, I would need a DNA sample from his son for confirmation. A one-to-one identical match as the final evidence."

"I get it. Thanks."

"I'll send my report over right away," Ryan said. "Good luck."

"Yeah."

Flint headed back to her office. She had a lot of questions, so she started a list. The sky darkened even further as she worked. At seven, she closed the lid of her laptop and got up. She headed down the corridor to the south foyer where the bustle of the day had already begun. The desk sergeant was munching on a breakfast roll when she walked up to his podium.

"You caught me." He laughed. "What can I do for you this morning?"

"I would like to have a chat with Dr. Lane before you let him go."

"Yeah, I see you sent me the discharge form already," the desk sergeant said. "I know it's none of my business, but what's going on?"

"It's complicated," Flint said, her eyebrows furrowed with worry.

"No problem. He's awake."

The officer came around the side of the counter and made his way through the gate. They walked briskly down the hallway to the holding area. The desk sergeant's effort to make small talk failed at every turn, so after a while he gave up.

"There you go." He unlocked the door and left.

Flint stood in front of the cell. The moment she had been dreading since talking to Ryan was upon her, and there was no way to avoid it now. She grabbed the handle and opened the door. Dr. Lane was lying on the mattress with his hands under his head, staring at the ceiling. She hesitated and then strode in. The doctor turned his head.

"Well?"

"The discharge papers have been signed. You're free to go," Flint said.

"It was a shitty night." Dr. Lane sat up. "Do I have to do anything?"

"Just sign the papers and get your belongings. But I would like to have a word with you before you go."

"Really?"

"Dr. Lane, I have some bad news for you," Flint said. "I'm not sure there's an easy way to say this." She sat on the lone chair.

"What? Has something happened to Shawn?"

"No. Nothing like that," Flint said.

"So, what's this about?"

"The DNA on the knife isn't yours."

"Okay. So, what's the problem here?"

"Half the markers of the DNA matched you." Flint paused. "We believe the DNA on the knife is from Shawn."

"What? That can't be right."

"He's your only son. You have no other children, right?"

"No. He's the only child," Dr. Lane said. "But why would Shawn even be in the study?"

"We'll have to bring him in to the station," Flint said. "We'll take a DNA sample for confirmation, then he'll be charged."

"Oh, God." Dr. Lane placed his head in his hands and moaned.

"I'm sorry," Flint said.

"It's not your fault." Dr. Lane stood up. "What's going to happen to him?"

Flint didn't answer, because she wasn't sure.

They walked to the foyer in silence.

The desk sergeant had everything ready for the doctor. After a few minutes, Dr. Lane stuck his keys and phone into his pocket. He turned to Flint.

"How much time have I got until the police come?"

"Let's make it for noon," Flint said. "Get him a good lawyer." She looked at him. "The best you can afford."

Dr. Lane nodded and strode out the door.

Flint walked slowly with heavy steps and a heavier heart. It might not be her fault, but she didn't feel comfortable arresting a juvenile for murder. Shawn hadn't turned seventeen, so he was still considered a youth in the justice system. But the truth of the matter was the courts could seek an adult sentence because of the magnitude of the crime. The only hope he had was for his lawyer to convince them the boy should be sentenced as a youth offender. So much depended on what the charges ended up being and on the extenuating circumstances. Once she charged Shawn with a crime and presented the reports to the prosecutor, he could do what he wanted with it. She would have no say in the end.

It would be a sobering moment for Shawn. A man had died. There was no way of getting around that. She would have another chat with Dr. Lane to drum into him the importance of his son being well represented. For her part, she would speak to Crown counsel and recommend leniency if it was warranted. But she wouldn't know that until she spoke to the boy and found out exactly what had happened.

Flint pushed all those thoughts aside, knowing she was getting a little ahead of herself. There was still work to do.

The most significant thing was confirming the DNA on the knife, although Ryan had left little doubt of the outcome.

The team was in the boardroom when Flint entered. She had sent a text, so they knew the score.

"Let's make this as painless as possible," Flint said. "I want Thornberry and Greenwood to pick Shawn up. Hay and I will go over our questions. His lawyer may tell him not to say anything, so we may not get any answers. But we'll just see how it goes." Flint looked over the stern faces. "Are we clear?"

"You bet, boss," Hay said.

The other two detectives nodded and shuffled out of the room.

Flint and Hay spent the next hour going over their material. A quick, sharp knock on the door made them look up.

"Everything is set." The desk sergeant loomed in the doorway. "What a lousy thing." He shook his head in dismay and turned away.

"You're telling me," Flint said.

With that the detectives strode down the hallway and met up with Thornberry and Greenwood who stood outside the interview room waiting for their next instructions.

"Did you get Shawn's blood sample to Ryan?" Flint asked.

"Yes, he's left for Nanaimo already," Thornberry said.

"I don't think this is going to take long," Flint said. "Get your reports finished. Let's wrap this up."

Flint entered the room. Dr. Lane, Shawn and a petite woman dressed in a well-tailored suit sat next to each other. The lawyer's briefcase was open on top of the table, and she had a notepad and pen in front of her.

With a quick nod, Flint sat down facing the trio. Hay took a seat beside the sergeant.

"Are we ready?" Flint asked.

"Yes," the lawyer said, with no embellishments.

"Okay." Flint turned on the recorder and introduced herself and the constable. "You will be representing the accused?"

"Yes. Mrs. Aubrey from Shell, Aubrey, James and Associates." Her matronly voice was warm and musical.

Flint thought she was perfect, the judge would love her.

"Okay. Your client is going to be charged for the death of Harris Crest. We spoke to Crown counsel this morning. He has agreed to hold back until this interview. So the charges laid will depend on the answers we get to our questions. Are we clear?"

Dr. Lane lowered his head.

"I believe it would be in my client's best interest to be forthcoming," Mrs. Aubrey said. "We intend to keep the trial in the youth justice system, so Shawn will answer whatever questions you have." She smiled with the same warmth her voice had portrayed.

Flint gazed at the young man, tilting her head, trying to get him to look her in the eye.

"Shawn. We don't believe you meant to kill Harris. Can you tell us what happened? Why did you go into the study?" Flint asked. "Take your time."

Shawn tugged at the collar of his shirt and swallowed. He raised his head and locked eyes with the sergeant.

"I was having a smoke down by the woods. Janice showed up all bent out of shape. She said my dad and Harris were arguing in the study. Something about my dad being a killer. So I went up there to see what was going on. By the time I got there my dad was gone. I would have left, but Harris said my dad was going to go to prison for what he did to his brother." Shawn drew in a breath. "I had no idea what the hell he was talking about. I pulled out my pocket-knife, waved it in the air and told him to piss off. He made like he was going to hit me, so I slashed at him. We got into a tussle, and then he fell backward. I figured he would be so mad that he would come after me, so I ran." Shawn let out a sob. "I didn't know he was dead. When I found out later, I didn't know what to do. I didn't mean..."

"Why did you toss the knife?"

"I don't know." Shawn shrugged. "Mostly because I thought my dad would give me shit for having it, I guess."

Flint looked up and saw Dr. Lane shaking his head. Shawn was probably right about that, she thought. His story was in line with her thinking. But the one glitch that could lead to more trouble for the boy was the fire. No matter what, her constable had almost been killed by the resulting explosion.

"Tell us about the fire." She spoke quietly.

"What? That wasn't me." His voice was steady.

They made eye contact, then Shawn glanced away.

Her instincts told her he was telling the truth. Like the key, it was just another distraction leading them in the wrong direction. But she knew that his buddies, Jim and the rest of them, would have to be brought in for questioning. She set those thoughts aside and concentrated on what was happening now.

"I'm satisfied Shawn had no malicious intent. That Harris's death was an accident." Flint gave the lawyer a nod. "Saying that, Shawn has to take responsibility for his actions."

"And he will," Mrs. Aubrey said. "What charge will Shawn be facing?"

"Manslaughter." The prosecutor had given her some latitude on the charge.

"I stand behind my son," Dr. Lane said.

"Okay. So that's it. We're done here. Shawn will be transferred to a youth detention centre until his first court appearance."

"He can't come home with me?" Dr. Lane asked.

Mrs. Aubrey touched his arm. "Shawn will be okay. I'll speak to Ray at the prosecution service and get this rolling."

"You have a good lawyer. Just do as she says, Shawn. Be patient," Flint said and stood up. So Mrs. Aubrey had a friend in high places, she thought and smiled. At the door, she turned around. "Take care."

Shawn's face had paled considerably, and his eyes had teared up. But there was also the look of fierce determination in the set of his jaw that he would see it through and come out the other side a better person.

Chapter 27

The detectives walked along the empty hallway, and for good reason Flint was glad of the silence and peacefulness. It had been a long, winding road to here. Like dominoes, one thing someone did triggered the next thing, and the next, and so on until someone had died. Where had it started? Was it Mrs. Crest for keeping a journal and laying bare her soul? Was it Harris and his threatening way with people? Trying to blame his older brother's death on Dr. Lane. Or Janice who had sent Shawn to the study, a boy who feared losing his dad?

"Charging Shawn with manslaughter instead of murder was the right call," Hay said.

"I think so."

Flint had no lingering doubts. She had sensed the love between father and son. Between Dr. Lane and Shawn. As her mind wandered more, she thought about Charles and Bryson. There was a strong connection between them, even before the birth certificate made its appearance. That was another push of the domino. Without the time capsule getting dug up before its time, there was the strongest of possibilities that Charles would have lived his life and never known about his other son. She sighed deeply.

"Are you okay?" Hay asked.

"Yeah, great actually." Her cell phone pinged. Flint scanned the screen, then put it back in her pocket. "That was from Ryan. He has confirmed it is Shawn's DNA on the knife."

They stopped in front of the boardroom. A murmur of voices slipped from under the doorway. And then a roar of laughter.

"What the hell?" Hay asked. He opened the door.

There were several boxes and a lot of beer bottles on the table. Thornberry sat at the far side with Jarrett beside her. He looked a little more human now. Greenwood munched on a slice of pizza and waved with her free hand. Neil turned around and looked over his shoulder to the new arrivals.

"I didn't know if you guys had anything to eat today. So I brought the refreshments," he said.

"Perfect." Flint grabbed a plate and helped herself to some food. Neil cracked open a beer for her.

"Are you coming back to the job after we did all the work, Jarrett buddy?" Hay asked.

"Not exactly," the constable said. He pulled out a letter and placed it on the table. With his hand, he pushed it over to Flint. "May as well let everyone know at the same time."

"Your resignation?" Flint asked.

Jarrett shrugged. "I'm not cut out for this. I've already used up two lives and it's just the beginning of my career."

Greenwood's eyes lit up. She glanced at the sergeant.

"What are your plans?" Flint asked.

"I still have a few months of rehab." He rubbed at his shoulder.

Flint nodded.

"I'll miss you, buddy," Hay said.

"And yes. Greenwood, we would love for you to stay on the team," Flint said.

"Thanks."

"So tomorrow we'll get our reports finished," Flint said.

She gave them the details of how the interview with Shawn had gone. Everybody seemed pleased enough with it, except for the fact that a young boy had screwed up royally.

They chattered, ate and drank and talked about normal stuff. Suddenly Flint jumped out of her chair.

"I have a few calls to make. Be right back."

She slipped out of the room. The first call was to her dad, to let him know she would be home in a few hours. They would talk, but she was doing well. The next call was to the superintendent. He was concerned for the Lane family but figured it would work out. And he was most pleased with the news that his niece would be staying on the major crime team.

Flint sat back down beside the mayor.

"Everything all right?" he said.

"So that's it. See you guys tomorrow," Flint said. She put Jarrett's letter in her pocket and stood up. He had made the right decision about quitting the force.

Neil grabbed her hand and gave it a squeeze as they walked to the front entrance.

"There's one more thing I need to do," Flint said.

Neil snickered.

"What?" She punched his arm. "Take me to the castle."

"Okay. Anything to make you happy."

They hopped into his vehicle and sat in silence on the long road up.

"Is this official?"

"Let's say it is."

Neil pulled into the portico and turned off the ignition.

"Show me the way," he said.

They headed up the steps. Flint steered them over to the study.

"Harris had a journal that he showed Dr. Lane. He said it had the proof that the doctor was guilty," Flint said. She tore away the police ribbon and unlocked the door. After switching on the light, they entered the room.

The study was as beautiful as she remembered from her brief visit here. The smell of lemon polish, the shine on the oak desktop and the smooth feel of the leather couches.

Flint strolled over to the built-in bookcase. The first time she had looked, all she saw were the large number of first edition books. This time she noticed the journals. There were three of them, each with the same binding as the ones in the cottages. She pulled one that had been pushed back in its place as if in a hurry, not quite in line.

Flint sat in a chair by the fireplace with the journal on her lap.

Neil sat in the armchair across from her.

Flint flipped through a few pages. A newspaper clipping, yellowed with age, fluttered to the floor. She picked it up and read it slowly.

"Is it about his brother, John?" Neil asked.

"Yes." Flint stuck the clipping back in the book. "It mentions Dr. Lane being with him, although he wasn't a doctor then. It was declared an unintentional drowning. That's pretty straightforward. So I'm not sure what got into Harris's head."

Neil nodded.

"This is one of his mother's journals." Flint turned to the last few pages. "The date here is just days before she died."

Neil crossed his arms and sat quietly while Flint read. After she finished, she looked up.

"Did you find something?"

"No. Absolutely nothing. Her last two entries are about how much she wished things had gone differently. She missed John. There's nothing laying any blame on the doctor. It's a tragedy Harris read something into it that just isn't here. She turned to the last page. "Haiku."

"What's that?"

"Sort of like a poem. A brief moment in time." A wistful look crossed over her face.

Flint read the first one out loud.

A giant wave!
A boy rides in—
Another waits forever on the shore.

"Jesus. Poor mother." Flint choked up for a sec, holding back the hurt. "Maybe Harris read this and thought that Dr. Lane should have swam out to rescue his brother. But he was wrong. How would he have known that John was in trouble?" She paused. "Actually, I think his mother was saying that Dr. Lane waited for his friend who never showed up and felt the sadness too."

She read the second one to Neil.

A special key.
A hidden door—
A family treasure unexpected and revealed.

"That'll be Bryson. The real treasure was the boy." Flint cried openly now.

Neil went over and held her tight.

"Everything will be okay."

List of Characters

RCMP Sergeant Marlowe Flint
Paige – her daughter
Bodhi – her dog
Victor Sullivan – her dad
Oleane Sullivan – her mom
RCMP Corporal Naomi Thornberry
RCMP Constable Gordon Hay
RCMP Constable Dennis Jarrett
RCMP Constable Patricia Greenwood
RCMP Superintendent Allen Gill
Dr. Kelly Churchman – pathologist from the BC Coroners Office
Ryan Harper – forensic scientist
Charles Crest – owner of Crest Castle
Harris Crest – his son
Paulie Webb – manager at castle
Neil Parson – the mayor
Dr. Chester Lane
Shawn Lane – doctor's son
Bryson Williams – real estate developer
Martha Williams – his wife
Kim Weaver – waitress

Mia Shaw – waitress
Janice Jenkins – apprentice gardener
Leanne Abbot – witness
Paula Wilkes – owner of the Seabreeze Cafe
Tim Miles – fire chief
Ken Moore – lawyer
Mrs. Aubrey – lawyer

If you enjoyed this book, please let others know by leaving
a quick review on Amazon. Also, if you spot anything
untoward in the paperback, get in touch. We strive for the
best quality and appreciate reader feedback.

editor@thebookfolks.com

More in this series

THE ALLEY (Book 1)

A gunshot rings out through a small Vancouver Island town. A man is dead in the jewelry store. Detective Marlowe Flint must work out if it was a robbery gone wrong, or an organized hit. But witnesses are reluctant to come forward, and when another man is beaten to within an inch of his life, the killer may slip through the detective's grasp.

Also by Kathy Garthwaite

MURDER ON VANCOUVER ISLAND
(Book 1)

Inspector Gibson cuts short a jaunt in his beloved kayak to attend a murder inquiry. The investigation soon meets a brick wall, but he suspects the victim's co-workers are involved. He must act quickly before the case, like the weather, goes cold.

MURDER AT LAKE ONTARIO
(Book 2)

The veteran detective is flown out to the east of the
country to help set up a major crimes task force. He soon
has a murder on his hands when a local shopkeeper is
found dead on the beach. Estranged from his melancholic
wife, Gibson's loyalties become divided.

MURDER ON THE SAANICH PENINSULA
(Book 3)

When a woman is murdered, Inspector William Gibson
immediately suspects her husband is responsible. His
junior partner is not so sure. But when the truth emerges it
has a knock-on effect that will change the detective's life
for ever. And not in a good way.

Other titles of interest

PROTECTION RACKET
by James Warren

When a hot-shot, womanizing lawyer is found murdered in his office, a female co-worker is indicted for the crime. Her parents call on David Lee from a rival firm to clear Amanda's name and defend her at trial. Falling for his attractive client, David will dig deep to prove her innocence, but there may be more to it than first meets the eye.

THE OTHER DETECTIVE
by James Davidson

Days before World War Two, Polish detective Johann Tal is called out to investigate a brutal murder. A couple have been discovered dead in Danzig's dockyards, and a policeman's bloodied uniform found next to them. Many years later, another detective is called out to a different murder. If the two cases are linked, it spells serious danger.

THE DEVIL'S ARTIST
by Iain Henn

When a massive wreck on the interstate kills several people, a mural in Seattle that seems to glorify the disaster creates outcry. However, upon discovering that the painting was created days before the event, criminal investigators are baffled. Are they dealing with a psychic artist, or someone who played a role in the incident? Soon other murals appear, and the race is on to stop further tragedy.

All FREE with Kindle Unlimited and available in paperback!

www.ingramcontent.com/pod-product-compliance
Lightning Source LLC
Chambersburg PA
CBHW032003180726
48283CB00008B/2553